CW01375882

Capricious Paradise

Caribbean Tales Told by Lis Twa

by
Gilliam Clarke

authorHOUSE™

1663 Liberty Drive, Suite 200
Bloomington, Indiana 47403
(800) 839-8640
www.AuthorHouse.com

This book is a work of fiction. People, places, events, and situations are the product of the author's imagination. Any resemblance to actual persons, living or dead, or historical events, is purely coincidental.

© 2005 Gilliam Clarke. All Rights Reserved.

No part of this book may be reproduced, stored in a retrieval system, or transmitted by any means without the written permission of the author.

First published by AuthorHouse 12/08/05

ISBN: 1-4208-5538-7 (e)
ISBN: 1-4208-5537-9 (sc)
ISBN: 1-4208-5536-0 (dj)

Library of Congress Control Number: 2005905104

Printed in the United States of America
Bloomington, Indiana

This book is printed on acid-free paper.

TABLE OF CONTENTS

Glossary of Caribbean Terms vi

Introduction vii

Scattergun 1

Nature Lovers 16

Tiki 29

Small Business 46

A Special Kind Of Hell 54

Miss Sally 63

Ramkissoon 73

Saved By The Bird 79

Dialogue 94

Yellowman 98

The Father Of His Country 106

GLOSSARY OF CARIBBEAN TERMS

Arse - the island word for one's behind
Beau vex - very angry
Callaloo - locally grown green leafy vegetable
Coolie - any person of East Indian descent
Copra - dried meat of the coconut
Crapaud - a poisonous toad
Cutlash - a blow, either psychological or from a weapon
Fete - any fun thing outside one's business
Garçon - man
Lambie - conch
Ligaroo - werewolf, from the French loup garou
Liming - 'hanging out'
Lis Twa - patois for 'the storyteller'
Makko - take a good look, check out thoroughly
Manicou - Caribbean possum
Mawga - small and inconsequential
Melogen - eggplant
Moko - stupid, dense, foolish
Petit quart - a half-pint of rum
Pickney - child or children
Shango - a sect that combines religion with white magic
Sweetie - small candy or a little gift
Tattoo - armadillo

INTRODUCTION

The eastern Caribbean is indeed a capricious paradise—nature has provided magnificent little islands, flowering trees and bushes whose beauty defies description, a tropical climate that is neither too hot nor too cold, a crystalline sea with beautiful beaches, mysterious, precipitous mountains covered with luxuriant vegetation—and not much else.

Fishing and farming are difficult. The tropical reef provides little that is edible, and the soil, while rich in some places, is far too thin in most areas for extensive farming.

Life is hard in the eastern Caribbean for most of the people. Those who live in the small cities suffer, as most city-dwellers do, from thieves, drug traffickers, stupidity, business corruption, and lazy, self-seeking politicians. But the people who live in the countryside, away from the direct pressure of the so-called civilizing influences, have developed their own way to cope with the limitations of poverty and restricted access to knowledge, which has been their lot since they were brought to the Caribbean from Africa as slaves, or from China and India as indentured laborers. The Europeans who fought one another for possession of these islands and exploited them have had little interest in the folks who have peopled them.

Except through a few Caribbean authors such as Naipaul, Lamming, and Walcott, these people aren't known to the American public, whose idea of the Caribbean has been shaped by works like Herman Wouk's tragicomic view "Don't Stop the

Carnival," and more recently in Bob Shacochis's macabre lyric, "Easy in the Islands." Each of these marvelously written books leaves one with the feeling that there is something vaguely sinister, something mysterious and unexplained—definitely foreign—about these islands and their inhabitants. This is inevitable, for the books express the views of outsiders who visit the islands.

This volume attempts to show the other point of view—some of the people's opinions and their views of the world outside and the way it functions. All of these stories, with the exception of "Nature Lovers," are based on the truth.

The central figure, Lis Twa (l'histoire or *storyteller* in patois), is used to focus attention on the interactions in rural communities, where even the eccentric old man cadging his drinks with dignity at the rum shop is part of the local process for teaching children some of the real values that make up community life: responsibility, obedience, courtesy, and respect. To appreciate the islands fully, such things must be known and understood.

It's to those back-country island people, with their humor that prevails in spite of the tragedies that sometimes dominate their lives, that this book is dedicated.

SCATTERGUN

Conversation was interrupted by a loud scream. The rum shop patrons crowded into the doorway and looked out. A woman standing naked in the center of the road hurled imprecations at the sky while she poured water from a calabash over her head and stamped her feet in fury.

"Who is she?" a Peace Corps worker asked.

"Dat's Crazy Marie," one of the farmers explained, turning back to the bar. "She get vexed because she don't have a mon, and she cuss de sky all de time." He shrugged. "Who gonna take on a woman like she? De mon have to be mad as well!"

Miss Lucy's rum shop was perched on a foundation of cement blocks placed at random under the rough floor. The walls were weathered gray boards nailed to uprights supporting a galvanized iron roof. No angle in the building was true; everything was just a little skewed, like Crazy Marie's mind.

Inside, a counter topped with cracked and worn linoleum tacked in place ran the length of the twenty-foot building and separated Miss Lucy from her customers. Behind her on the left were stacked tins of corned beef, milk, Vienna sausages, sardines, and a few tins of beans, along with packets of sugar and flour and Andrew's Liver Salts.

The Americans—Peace Corps volunteers and a civil engineer named Charlie Prudhomme—stood in the rum shop at sundown having a drink and chatting people up as was the custom before heading homeward for their evening meal.

They idly watched the ladies or, as was sometimes the case, children sent on errands, move in and out with their bits of bread, cheese, sardines, tinned beef—whatever they were having for tea. There was a rickety table behind the counter which held a half round of cheddar cheese, two large plastic jars of small candies, and several wood and glass cases filled with bread.

There was the usual laughter, chivvying—you know how men get on together after a day's work—when a sudden hush fell on the company.

Several children moved aside, giggling, to make room for a very elderly gentleman wearing beat-up jeans, a ragged shirt, and a straw hat with donkey's ears woven into it. The hat was festooned with freshly picked purple bougainvillea.

The foreigners in the rum shop looked at one another in puzzlement, never having seen the old man before. He appeared to be around ninety or so but well- preserved. His teeth, unfortunately, had not shared in the general preservation, and his gums gleamed within his smiling mouth.

"Lis Twa! Lis Twa," one of the children called, "tell we a story!"

The old man grinned toothlessly and pretended to swat the child on the rump. "Your mooma waiting for you, chile. She want de food in she house, not in your hand. Get yourself home before she come for you."

The child, laughing, skipped out the rum shop door and ran down the side of the road.

The right end of the building was reserved for the bar. Signs advertising Caribbean rums—Mount Gay, Cockspur, Old Oak, Clark's Court, Vat 19, and Bounty--decorated the walls along with the bottles set on a shelf.

"Gimme a rum, Miss Lucy," the chap said to the lady behind the bar. "A white rum." He licked his lips in anticipation.

"You have money, Mr. Flowers?" she asked crisply. She was a lovely brown-skinned woman in her fifties. Kindness and compassion were in her eyes.

"No, I have a story instead."

She passed him the rum. The regular denizens of the shop settled down to listen, so the Americans did the same. The children sat on the floor in front of the bar, watching Lis Twa.

The old man drank his rum straight off and chased it with a glass of water, which Miss Lucy provided from a covered bucket set on the counter for that purpose. She refilled his glass and smiled.

He looked around at the company, then sat on the one chair in the shop as if it were a throne. "All you remember dat *garçon* in Grenada by de name of Scattergun? Of course dat ain't he real name; dat's he false name. He real name is John Hippolyte.

"I always wonder why he named Scattergun—it a funny name for a mon to have—until one of he outside women tell me dat he called so because he have a lot of children. *Bon Dieu!* If you see children! She tell me he have three by she, and five by she best friend. De mon really named well, eh?

"Well, I hear dat Scattergun have fifty-three children in all, and he have about thirty outside women! Bwoy, de mon busy from morning until de night fall, *oui?*

"I knew Scatter in dose days. When I was young I worked for a time in Grenada. He live up in Tempe, in a real ratty cardboard shack—garbage around de yard, chicken on de roof. Scatter don't care about nothing at all but drinking rum and making baby. Of course he worked when he had to, but he really have to get down, *down* before he take on a job! He was kind of worthless, really, but de mon could charm a woman, *oui!*"

In the long pause that followed, his audience shifted and got more comfortable. Miss Lucy poured another round for everyone, then leaned over the bar. "Is that all there is to the story, Lis Twa?"

"No, Miss Lucy, but I dry."

"Let me buy you a drink, sir," said Charlie Prudhomme, the engineer.

"*Merci, garçon.*" The old fellow continued. "Well, Scattergun have he favorite woman, like all men. She named Gloria. And she pretty, pretty. To show de world she was he favorite, he gave she eight children by de time she was twenty-six. Dat is favorite, eh? 'Bwoy,' he would tell anyone who listen, 'you see me? I am a Caribbean mon—a real mon. I have plenty women, plenty children, and no responsibility! You ever see a mon who have it so good?' Sad t'ing is, a lot of men envy him. No responsibility is nice, *oui*?

"When he make a baby in a woman, after six months she don't see him for over a year because he consider babies a trial until dey walk. He just take up with de other outside women and do he t'ing.

"Well, Scatter living so and drinking up in de rum shop every night until God decide to teach him a lesson. When God teach a mon, He teach well."

"Oh, Lord, Mr. Flowers," Miss Lucy exclaimed, "tell the story, eh!" She tended two more customers, then came back to lean on the bar.

"You remember dat Hurricane Janet?" Mr. Flowers asked. "Well, Janet decide to visit Grenada dat year, but no one really believe de storm going to hit. Scatter in de rum shop one afternoon when he hear people talking about some storm, and he just laugh—he have a good, deep-down-in-de-belly laugh—and drink another rum. Den one of he children by Gloria come in de shop and pull on he shirt…"

"Mr. Scattergun, sah, Mooma really sick, and she ask me to come for you."

Scattergun was vexed. He didn't want any child pulling on his shirt, whining about a sick mother in front of all his friends. Some of his cronies down the bar were snickering already—behind their hands, of course. No one dared laugh at John Hippolyte to his face.

"Tell your mooma I busy, chile. Go on. Now!"

"But, Mr. Scatter, Mooma bent over, and she crying! De nurse say she must have operation, or she going to die!"

The child looked so forlorn that Scatter began to feel uncomfortable. He shrugged his shoulders carelessly and looked at his drinking mates. "Operation sound bad, eh?"

"Bwoy, operation sound like death!" one of them replied.

Scatter shuffled his feet in the dust on the floor, studied the ceiling for a bit, then downed his rum in one gulp. "Well, I better go see what wrong with Gloria, if she dat sick. Chile, you go tell your mooma I'll drop in just now."

Some chap down the bar tittered. "Scatter, de woman cotch you f'sure! You always talking about how you give women present when you make dem a baby. Well, she giving you de message back, eh, *garçon?*"

"Eight of dem," someone else said, laughing.

Scattergun pushed away from the bar and snorted. "You shut dat mouth, *garçon*, else I shut it for you! And keep you nose out my business, understand?" Shoulders high, he stalked from the rum shop.

Gloria's house sat on the edge of a deep ravine. It had a beautiful view of the city of St. Georges across the mountains. The Caribbean Sea sparkled like some rare jewel between the green peaks.

Overhead the sky was a clean-swept deep blue. Birds sang in the trees. Grackles screamed at one another from shanty roofs along the path.

Scatter liked Gloria's house. It was twelve by twenty feet, plenty big, and cool in the rainy season, with a constant breeze. And she kept it well. She worked hard to make a home for her children. A Canadian gentleman hired her year-round to see to his house on Grand Anse and paid her a handsome five dollars a day…

Three small children sneaked into Miss Lucy's rum shop now and settled in a corner. Their eyes shone in the dim light. They were mouse quiet. Miss Lucy looked hard at them, and they lowered their eyes, pretending they hadn't seen her.

"Mooma know you here, children?" she asked.

"Yes, Miss Lucy," they responded shyly.

"All right, then." She turned to Mr. Flowers. "Another rum, Mr. Flowers?"

"No, not now, thank you, Miss Lucy. A little water would be nice." He went on. "Well, Gloria really sick. She have appendicitis and must go for operation, one time. She beg Scatter to stay with de children until she out of de hospital. He didn't want to do it, but she have no one else to leave de children with. She family live all de way up in Sauteurs..."

Scatter stayed. The district nurse bustled Gloria off to the hospital in St. Georges, and he was left with the children. He didn't know where to begin or what to do. Except for the eldest child, Susan, he did not even remember their names.

The next morning found Scattergun in the yard, washing baby clothes. The children brought him buckets of water from the standpipe down the path. He rinsed the diapers carelessly, then draped them to dry on hibiscus bushes in Gloria's front yard.

"Morning, Mr. Scatter," called one of the neighbors from across the path. "You hear about de storm?"

"What storm you talking, Mary?" he yelled over his shoulder.

"Hurricane coming! Me in de rum shop to get some cheese dis morning, and dey say dat Hurricane Janet suppose to hit Grenada dis very day!" She came across the path, her arms crossed over her breasts, and watched Scattergun intently. "Dem diaper ain't rinse properly. De baby get a rash—"

"Shut you mouth, woman," Scatter threatened.

She shrugged. "Anyway, dey say we must put food in de house and get in de goat and chicken."

"Dey a bunch of old women," he scoffed. "Hurricane! We ain't never had hurricane in Grenada, don't you know dat? How hurricane gonna hit we?" He turned his back on Mary and went on washing clothes.

Resigned, she left to tend her business.

Later that day the wind began to blow hard. Scatter rushed around the yard to gather the baby's clothes before they blew away. He looked across the mountains to St. Georges and the sea. A bruised pall, puffy and black, hung over the horizon. Whitecaps formed, and waves began to roll into the Carenage, the harbor around which St. Georges was built. Scatter set about closing up the house. It looked as if they were in for a bad rain.

The children, meanwhile, were in turmoil. They missed their mother. Scatter was worried because the district nurse had not returned. He didn't know if Gloria was alive or dead.

What in God's name would happen if she died? he wondered. Was he supposed to look after the bloody children for the rest of his natural life? He was already tired of carrying the baby around. Twice he started down the hill to the nurse's house, and twice he had to turn back because the baby began screaming and yelling and carrying on. Nothing could quiet her. Scatter was desperate.

By late afternoon, the storm was upon them. The air lay as heavy on his soul as had the thought of working. Scatter opened the shutter facing away from the wind. Looking out, he saw roofs flying through the air. Coconuts whistled by like cannonballs. A giant mango tree crashed to the ground in the yard across the street, wrecking Mary's house. Mary went crying down the path and was knocked over by a piece of galvanized sheeting. She staggered to her feet and ran away.

The house chattered, shaking with the terrific force of the gusts. The roof screamed when the wind hit it, and the floor shook like a wounded bird.

The children were frightened out of their wits. The seven younger ones huddled in the center of the room. They bawled and screamed for an end to the din outside.

"God, chile, can't you stop de baby crying?" Scatter yelled at Susan. "De damn chile sound like *ligaroo!*"

"I'll try, Poopa," the eldest whined. "But I scared, Poopa!"

Scatter was indignant. "What you mean, calling me Poopa? Where you respect? All you call me Mr. Scattergun, you hear? Storm ain't no reason to call me Poopa!"

"Why did he object to being called Poopa?" one of the Peace Corps volunteers asked Mr. Flowers. "I don't understand."

"Well, *garçon,* if no chile call you Poopa, you ain't have no chile." The old man smiled softly. "You buying me another rum?"

"Sure thing," the young man answered.

Miss Lucy gave Mr. Flowers his refill, and he drank it down. She then poured rounds for all and topped off the water glasses. The children who had come to listen to Lis Twa moved from their corners and now were sitting in the middle of the floor. They gazed with awe at Lis Twa as he continued.

"Well, de storm get worse, and Gloria house feel like it doing some devil dance on de hillside. De children reach de point where dey too scared to cry or move anymore, so dey just cringe in a corner and whine. All except de baby, and dat chile have a set of lungs dat could be heard from St. Georges to Carriacou!

"Den all dem get hungry and ask Scatter, where de food? He in a spot, because dere ain't no food in de house..."

Scatter was almost out of his mind. The children were yowling from fear and bawling for food, but there wasn't a bite in the house. Twice he checked the food safe, but emptiness stared at him from behind the screen mesh.

Susan went to her father. "You want me to go to de rum shop and get a little food, Mr. Scatter, sah?"

"No, chile, de weather too bad. I'll go. You stay right here in de house and look after de children until I get back, eh? And none of you go outside de house, you hear?"

He glanced at Gloria's daughter, which was how he thought of her, and felt something akin to pity. She was trembling, but she went to the other children and tried to comfort them.

Scatter went out into the storm. The wind took him as if he were a tiny bug, flattened him against a coconut tree, and smashed his nose. It began to bleed. Scatter cursed the storm and every living thing. He fought his way down the path to the rum shop. It was locked tight.

"Blighty!" he screamed to the owner and prayed his voice could be heard above the banshee wail of the wind. "God, mon, open de door!" He banged with his fists on the side of the shop and was rewarded when the door opened a little.

Blighty, eyes enormous with fright, peered out at Scatter. "Mon, what de ass you doing out in dis storm? You mad or what? Come in, quick, before de wind blow de damn door away!"

Scatter went inside. After the pandemonium outside, the relative quiet was eerie. "I need some food for Gloria's children, Blighty. Gimme ten breads and three tins of corned beef, and a big slice of cheese, in case dis damn wind continue. And better give me eight sweeties."

Blighty, shaking his head with wonderment, looked at Scattergun. "Mon, it better to stay in de house hungry dan come out in de hurricane. You get hit by tree, and you dead, one time!" He bundled up Scatter's purchases in brown paper and tied them with a string. "Sound to me like de wind getting worse, eh?" Blighty went to the door and peered out cautiously. "God, de house across de path just take off like plane, Scatter!" He ducked as a large sheet of galvanized roofing guillotined the door. "You better get back to de children. It getting worse for sure."

A tree next to the rum shop crashed to the ground, taking the roof with it. Scatter and Blighty ducked as overhead beams fell around their heads. Shelving in the rum shop split and popped, showering them with tins of beef, milk, and small bottles of rum.

Rain began to fall. It fell like a river from the leaden sky, slashing, bruising, beating bushes right into the ground.

The two remaining walls of the rum shop began to tremble. Scatter looked at Blighty and shouted, "Get to de church, mon!"

As Blighty took off, Scatter made a frantic run up the path to Gloria's house. Susan let him in the door, then the two of them fought to close it again. Rain on the roof turned their world to the inside of a giant drum.

The children were too terrified to eat. Scatter put most of the food in the safe for later. With his teeth he tore off a piece of bread and tried to chew, but it stuck in his throat. For the first time in his life, he was scared. There was no way to sweet-talk the monster raging outside...

Miss Lucy glanced at the children, then opened a Pepsi and poured the cola into small cups for them to share. She gave little Gemma the drinks to pass around to the other children. Each took a cup and held it, still staring with open mouth at Lis Twa.

Mr. Flowers nodded in satisfaction, and the donkey ears on his hat bobbed as he went on with his tale.

"Scatter now huddled in de corner with de children. De house bucking like a skittish young horse. De baby finally wore sheself out and gone to sleep. De other children crouch up, eyes bugged out, and watched de straining galvanized sheets over dey heads..."

Scatter hit his forehead with the heel of his palm. He should have gotten himself a *petit quart* of rum when he went for the food. Then he'd have some comfort now while the wind roared outside instead of having to sit and stare at children who were frightened out of their wits. They made him realize how afraid he was.

Gloria had no right to ask this of him! They were *her* children, not his. He could be at a rum shop in St. Georges now, drinking up with the boys, laughing at the storm.

Suddenly he realized that he could hear the children's whimpering again. He listened. There was quiet outside. He leaped to his feet and flung open the front door—just as the worst winds hit.

Everything in the house moved. Pots and pans went skidding up the walls. The door burst open. A chair staggered across the room and crashed out into the night. Gloria's bed, against the wall, began a lunatic waltz toward the door. The children, dodging flying debris, yelped with terror.

An evil sound filled their ears. *Whump!* Then the house was no more; the roof planed away into the witless void. The walls shrieked and peeled away, then skittered across the yard.

Rain beat the children like a cruel master. It rained so hard they were blinded. And the noise! A sound like ten thousand jet engines screeched through the howling dark. Suddenly the children vanished.

Scatter didn't know what to do. His mashed nose hurt like hell. He could see nothing. How did children fly? Where were they? Nothing was left of Gloria's house but the floor, and as he crouched, that began to tilt under him.

He flung himself to the ground as the floor cartwheeled away. Scatter struggled to his feet, then stood, bewildered, staring after it.

Something slammed into the side of his head and knocked him flat. He groaned, lying in the mud, stupid from the blow.

"Mr. Scattergun, sah, you got to get up! Mr. Scatter, sah!" It was Susan. She clung to a tree in the yard. When her father fell, she dropped to her knees, then to her stomach, and bellied against the wind to where he lay.

Scatter pulled himself to a sitting position and grabbed the girl. "Susan, where de children?"

"I got Mary and Jennie and Rob and Henry. Pope and Mercy are over dere. But de baby gone, Poopa. De poor baby gone!" She burst into tears.

Scatter climbed painfully to his feet. Lurching against the wind, he began a search in the screaming blackness surrounding them. Susan held on to his pants. Scatter and Susan battled back and forth, beaten and sliced by unseen missiles. Finally they reached Pope and Mercy, who were clinging for dear life to a fallen sugar apple tree at the very edge of the ravine. Somehow he got them down the path to the church, which was still standing...

"Oh, God, de poor baby!" little Gemma cried.

The other children hushed her and shrank back into silence, lest they be told to go home in the middle of Lis Twa's story.

"Miss Lucy, dis de third time I ask you for a tin of beef," snapped a lady who stood at the far end of the counter. "Me hungry, and you standing dere listening to dat old mon!"

Miss Lucy sighed with elaborate patience, then went to serve the hag. The woman left, muttering under her breath, her purchase wrapped and perched on her head.

"Well, Scatter know he have to find dat baby," Mr. Flowers continued. "He know how Gloria dote on de chile, because she tell Scatter it de last. She taking some new t'ing called birth control.

"He don't have any idea where to begin to look, but he remember de other children on de edge of dat ravine, so he decide, if God spare, to try looking dere…"

The wind had torn away the world. Scatter was lost in the howling gloom. Nothing was left standing to guide him.

The rain beat against his squinted eyes and tried to snatch them out. A tree branch flew by, lashing his head. He fell into the mud again. He looked up to curse the limb and saw a galvanized sheet incising the air where he had been. Scatter began to shake like one of his children. He sat in the muddy night, mauled by flying debris, and wondered how he was still alive. His brain ached. Reality was ripped apart. Then he had an awesome thought: suppose he had been spared because he had to find Gloria's child. He felt strange, thinking like that, strange and small.

He stood and tried to search along the edge of the ravine, but no one could walk in that wind; it was blowing, he guessed, at over a hundred and fifty miles an hour. Scatter was knocked to his knees by another unseen missile. He crawled, dodging coconuts, branches, pots, clothes, soursops, and breadfruit. Everything in Grenada was airborne in the night.

He worked his way a little distance down the ravine side and was hunting behind everything he could find when he heard a roar that obliterated the sound of the storm. Frozen, he looked over his shoulder. A wall of water raced toward him, carrying bits of houses and trees. Frantic, Scatter tried to climb. But the water took him.

Washed to the bottom of the ravine, Scatter grabbed a branch and caught hold of it. His helter-skelter rush halted with a bone-jarring snap. Panting and spewing water, he looked up. A giant breadfruit tree, tumbling in the raging flood, bore down on him. He screamed as he was ripped from his branch and thrown back into the water.

He went under. Holding his breath, he fought madly to surface. He was angry now—there was no reason he should be treated so! He refused to drown. Branches tore at his clothing. Rocks smashed him. He grew faint. His thoughts grew dark and peaceful. Then he found the surface. Like flotsam, he was borne down the raging torrent while the wind tore up Creation above his head.

Just when he felt he could stay afloat no longer, he fetched up hard against a large boulder in the water's path. His breath *whooshed* from his body. He couldn't move.

Flattened like wet paper against the boulder, he watched another giant rock barreling down the ravine toward him. He knew he was going to die. Miraculously, the giant stone stopped two feet in front of him and diverted the flow of water. Weak and battered, he dragged himself up the ravine wall.

"Thank you, Jesus, for dis, my life." For the first time in his life Scatter uttered a fervent prayer.

The roar and frenzy of the water increased. It rose dangerously where he crouched. He had to get out. His fingers were raw and bleeding as he painfully clawed his way up the almost perpendicular wall. His head felt as though it would topple from his neck. He inched up the muddy slope.

An overhanging tree above him crashed down, knocking him sideways. He slipped then, slid in impossible positions, clutching at the greasy ground and howling with fear.

His thighbone snapped as he collided with a huge rock. The pain paralyzed him. He dropped headlong into the whirling torrent.

He surfaced again and gasped with pain. "God, why You trying to kill me so?" he screamed as his body hurtled farther down the ravine. He was close to the sea now and would certainly be washed out into the storm and drowned.

Suddenly the current swirled. He was bobbing around like a ball in a pool but was alive. Scatter looked around in wonder. All the houses from the top of the ravine were piled up in a narrow defile, making a dam.

Grunting with agony, he dog-paddled slowly to the edge of the water and clawed his way onto the mud. He lay panting, wanting to die. The pain in the leg was too much to bear. Each time he moved, the bone ends grated against each other. Gnashing his teeth, he forced himself to move away from the edge of the dam.

Then he heard it—a mewling cry over by the flotsam.

"What dat?" he called. Then he heard it again—a baby's crying.

He looked up at the clouds scudding across the sky. Dawn was breaking. In its thin light he saw that some trees were standing, triumphant still, but their tops were bent in a lashing frenzy as the wind tore through.

"God, please let dat be my baby!" Scatter lay for a long time in the wreckage listening to the baby squall. He was exhausted, in agony, but he gathered himself and began to drag his pain-racked body across the sodden debris...

"Oh, no, Lis Twa!" Miss Lucy breathed. "What happened to that poor man?"

"Poor *man?*" one of the Peace Corps fellows jeered. "He deserved everything he got! What about the poor baby?"

Mr. Flowers grinned. "Mon, I dry. All dis storying give a mon a thirst, you know."

Charlie Prudhomme bought Mr. Flowers a rum and leaned forward eagerly to hear the end of the tale.

Mr. Flowers toasted his benefactor, downed the drink at one gulp, took a sip of water, then wiped his lips, dragging out the moment as long as he decently could.

"At last Scatter find de baby. He thank God and drag de child to where he lying. He pulled de baby onto he stomach, den Scatter faint..."

Sometime later, he came to himself and saw that the child was asleep on his belly. The baby didn't seem to be badly hurt, just bruised and wet. Scatter looked at the tiny girl, then noticed for the first time that she had feet and hands shaped just like his own.

The infant woke, smiled, then lifted her arm and touched Scattergun's face. She had the same little stubborn dimple in her chin that marked Scatter's face when he smiled. She made some tender noise, and Scatter began to weep because then he remembered the child's name: Johnna Hippolyte.

Miss Lucy wiped tears from her eyes. "Then what happened?"

"Bwoy, Scatter reform! We find him and de baby next morning about ten, when de wind gone and sun shining like it brand new in de sky. Scatter have fever, and he real sick. But he holding dat chile like it he life.

"If you see Grenada, it mash up from end to end! All de islands, Carriacou, Petit Martinique, Union—de whole of de Grenadines—cotch hell when Miss Janet come to call.

"Well, when Scatter and Gloria get out de hospital dey marry, one time. He even get a job! Dey apply for one of dem precut houses de Americans send down after de hurricane, and he become a real family mon."

Mr. Flowers stood up and bowed toward Miss Lucy as if he were a courtier. "I thank you for de rum, my lady."

"The pleasure was ours, Lis Twa," she responded formally.

Then he turned to the Americans and bowed again. "And thanks to you, *garçons*." Before any of them could speak, he hobbled out the door and off into the gentle dark.

Miss Lucy sighed. "God works in mysterious ways, *oui?*"

The Peace Corps workers made ready to leave as well. Charlie turned to Miss Lucy. "Who is that grand old man?"

"He is rather special, isn't he?. He loves to have his rum in the evenings and to tell the children stories, Mr. Charlie. I encourage him. It's good for the little ones."

"Not only for the children, Miss Lucy. I'll have to budget for more drinks; I can see that. Good night, then."

"Good night, gentlemen, until tomorrow..."

NATURE LOVERS

Charlie Prudhomme, the civil engineer, and Dana Martin, one of the Peace Corps workers, stopped and stared at the rum shop. Miss Lucy was standing in the doorway, hands on her hips, and glaring at a couple getting into a rental car. As the car sped away, Miss Lucy tramped back inside. Charlie and his friend followed and met Mr. Flowers just inside the door. Charlie took the old man's arm and led him aside. "What made Miss Lucy so angry?" he asked.

Mr. Flowers's eyes twinkled. "Miss Lucy vex, vex! De people two English tourist, and de woman shout she don't want no drink in such a place. De glass here going be dirty, she say. Dere ain't no table for she to sit by--you know how some tourist get on. Miss Lucy tell de woman dis a poor mon's drinking place, and if she don't like it so, den she can get she arse back to de Hilton!" He chuckled, then looked over his shoulder. "Bwoy, I always find dat when I vex with someone, de best way to feel good again is to do dem back. You watch me make Miss Lucy smile!" He led Charlie back into the shop and up to the counter.

"Let me buy you a rum, sir," Charlie offered.

Miss Lucy, overhearing, reached awkwardly for the bottle, almost knocking it over. Muttering to herself, still furious, she slopped the rum into a shot glass and passed it to the old story teller. Then she poured Charlie a beer.

After drinking his usual, Mr. Flowers sat in the chair and gazed at the assembled company: three farmers from the area who were laughing uproariously over Miss Lucy's reaction to the English, several local ladies who had stopped in for their tea makings, and the usual assortment of children. When it became apparent that Lis Twa was about to tell a tale, the gathering shifted its attention to him.

"Today I gonna tell all you about some English. You know how dey come to we island and go into de rain forest? Well, some year ago, four of dem go in, but only <u>one</u> come out!"

The children gasped collectively, and their little eyes shone with curiosity.

"Eh-eh, garcon, dem English almost lose one today to Miss Lucy, oui?" one of the farmers asked, chuckling.

"Damn right!" Another of the men raised his glass in a toast to Miss Lucy, who was still fuming. "Let dem pay five dollar for a rum if dey want! Dis a poor mon's drinking place, thank de Lord, and we can still get a rum for twenty-five cent!"

"What happen to de other English, Lis Twa?" little Gemma asked, leaning forward and touching the old man's knee.

"Mr. Flowers, tell the tale," Charlie urged, sipping his beer.

"Dis driver I know from Castries, he name Guy, tell me dat he take Lady Jane Frowith and she husband, Sir Percy, to de forest trail. Dey had another couple, some woman Lady Jane like to mash up on--name Pamela. She husband called Henry Daedalus. All you remember Lady Jane, how hard she was in de head? After Guy warn so dey don't get lost or in trouble, de woman decide she must do she own t'ing."

A farmer laughed. "Me hear she bounce up on de lizard."

"What lizard?" Dana was curious.

"Mon, you never hear about de lizard up on Mount Gimi?" Mr. Flowers asked, incredulous. "He have a long, long tail, and he big as a barracks."

"Oh, come now," Dana scoffed.

Mr. Flowers looked at Gemma. "You tell dem, chile. Dey don't believe me."

"De lizard as big as a house, sah," she confirmed solemnly.

"Eh-*ehhhhh!*" Charlie replied…

"Here we are, sah." Guy turned in his seat and smiled toothily as his four passengers climbed down from the van. "De trail begin here and go up into de mountains. You sure you want to go without a guide? I be glad to take all you."

"Had we needed a guide, I would have engaged someone from the Naturalists' Society," Lady Jane snapped, surveying the driver with distaste. She obviously expected him to unload their gear. She looked sourly at her husband. "Oh, Percy, do hurry! You'll fiddle the day away with all this waffling. Here's your hat. Put it on."

"Jane, do be still. Dr. Flambeau told me that I should probably see the *jacquot* on this hike, and I want to be sure I have fresh film in the camera." Sir Percival continued painstakingly to reload his camera while Henry pulled their belongings from the van.

His wife glared at him, then at the others in the party, her pudgy face set like that of an irate hamster. "Pamela, are you certain you have everything? Is your canteen full?" She snatched the container from Pamela's belt and shook it, then handed it back.

"Yes, Jane, I'm ready and so is Henry. Percy, do hurry. Jane, do you have the waterproof?" Pamela asked anxiously. "I don't want to get my new perm wet."

"Yes, yes, I have the waterproof. Do you have a brolly?"

"Of course. Percy, *please!*" Pamela was eager to get moving.

But Sir Percival placidly returned his camera to its case, then removed his binoculars from theirs. He started polishing the lenses. "I shall be ready in a moment, Pamela. If you three wish to go ahead, I'll follow your trail, provided you don't go off it." He chuckled quietly at his own wit and began to polish the second lens. While doing so, he glanced with appreciation at the magnificent eucalyptus trees beyond, their bark a pastiche of rust, sherbet orange, brilliant green, and silvery tan…

"Now, all you know how de foreigner dress up, dress up when dey go into de forest," Mr. Flowers said. "Dey carry backpack, canteen--some I see even take tent! Dey don't t'ink dey in a real country here in de islands--a country with police, fire engine, all dat kind of t'ing. Dey in a hotel, and when dey leave de compound, dey t'ink dey going into some Tarzan movie, eh?" Mr. Flowers held out his empty glass, and Miss Lucy refilled it.

"Well, Lady Jane get on de driver--what time he going meet dem on de other side, if he gonna be on time, dat kind of t'ing. Guy tell me dey fitted out for a trek through de Sahara: canteen galore, backpack with dat new freeze-dried food, waterproof matches, raincoats, umbrellas. He say dey wouldn't carry de umbrellas in de Sahara, but dey could survive almost anywhere for a week. All dat for a six hour walk..."

"My God, Percy, are you ready? The morning is half gone!"

"Yes, my dear, I am ready to commune with nature." Sir Percival sighed, picked up his walking stick, and started through the bush. He turned and looked back at his party. "You are coming then, aren't you, Jane?"

"Mmmppff!" came the indignant reply. Lady Jane pushed Pamela and Henry ahead of her, took three steps into the bush, then turned to the driver again. "Now, driver, be sure you are on time."

"Yes, Lady Jane. Enjoy your day."

"I shall want a thermos of hot tea at the end of the trail, and Percy will want whiskey. Pamela and Henry will just have to make do."

"Yes, Lady Jane. Oh, by de way, if you run into any elephants, don't panic."

"Don't be ridiculous! This is St. Lucia, not Africa!"

"Dat's what I meant. Have a good hike." The driver shrugged, put the van into reverse, then backed down the track until he could turn the vehicle around. He switched off the engine and sat for a few moments, relishing the quiet, wishing that the elephant were not in a different part of the island, so that Lady Jane might encounter it.

Another of the British had, some years before and for reasons known only to himself and God, shipped a young female elephant to St. Lucia. She was put in the rain forest between the Pitons, to live out her lonely life swimming to yachts anchored in the lovely bay there, begging food, and being harassed by the native Lucians, who looked upon her as a jest.

Tourists amused Guy, the exceptions being the Lady Janes of the world. He remembered some visitors for years, likable people who thoroughly enjoyed the island and its beautiful beaches. Most vacationers never left those beaches to seek the wild wonder of the interior, where flowering trees against the blue of the sky were almost an electric shock to the eye— where foliage encompassing every shade of green tumbled down rocky slopes in giant cascades to end in a froth of pink and white blossoms and the delicate tracery of ferns.

Guy, having watched as Sir Percy retreated into the quiet of his mind, away from the bullyragging of Lady Jane's voice, felt an overwhelming kinship with the Englishman. He knew that Sir Percival had sought the *jacquot* for years but was unable to find the shy little parrot that hid in the rain forests. Since the Englishman's first visit to the island years before, the *jacquot's* numbers had dwindled. Now they were an endangered species—both the parrot and poor Sir Percy.

Far away from Guy and his thoughts, Lady Jane's party walked for an hour without incident, Percy foraging ahead and to one side of them in search of the rare *jacquot*. Thus far, having seen only a kingbird and a finch, he was disappointed.

He sat on a boulder and looked around him. Down the track he could hear the rest of the party plunging like a small herd through the deep, leafy silence. His wife's irritating voice played off-key against a counterpoint of slashing sounds as she beat the tropical foliage into submission with her stick. Lady Jane attacked life as if it were the enemy.

Strange how sound echoed in wild places, Sir Percy mused. Human voices assumed fairylike qualities quite beautiful at a distance. The exception was his wife's, which was strident even when muted, echoing forever in the corners of his mind, hectoring, endlessly yapping.

A bird's cry broke into his reverie. He looked around for it. Ah, yes, there on that branch sat a pearly-eyed thrasher. Percy loved its song. Cautiously he brought out his camera and telescopic lens, then fitted them carefully together. The bird, as if aware of his intent, sat still and watched him, its head cocked to one side. He got a lovely shot.

"Percy! Percy, where are you!" came his wife's querulous cry.

Muttering, he stood up. "I'm over here, to your left."

She burst through the bush. "This trail is boring. Why don't we get off it and do our walking in some place untouched by other visitors?"

"The driver warned us about that, Jane, and I'm sure he won't want to spend two or three hours waiting for us if we get lost." Sir Percival was disinclined toward great physical effort even when in England. The heat and humidity of the islands left him limp.

"Damn the driver!" Lady Jane puffed and huffed, then cast about like a dog seeking a scent. She left the trail and started up a steep incline. "Are you coming?" she called imperiously. "It is gorgeous up here! Come, Pamela! Henry, come." When Lady Jane looked back toward Sir Percival, her nose wrinkled with disgust. "Percy, are you joining us, or shall we meet you at trail's end?" Then she turned and climbed again.

He could hear her thrashing through the bush, beating at broad-leaved things. It was such a temptation to walk on, to enjoy the peace of the wild without his wife's nattering. But habit prevailed. "Jane, I shall protect the rear."

Her derisive laughter drifted down to him.

The incline steepened. The climb took all their breath and energy; talk was simply out of the question, for which Percy was profoundly grateful. He glanced over his shoulder to judge just how far they had come from the trail and caught his breath.

He was in an open place, able to see over the surrounding trees. There were vast panoramas. The Caribbean Sea stretched endlessly into the distant haze; no horizon was defined. Indeed, it seemed that he could view the entire world laid before him like a mirage shimmering under a perfect sky. The forest below was a composite of amethyst, sapphire, and emerald hues—here and there sparked the brilliant ruby of some flowering tree. He laid down his stick and, lost in the beauty lying at his feet like a sweet, complaisant woman, went to work with his camera. He quite forgot his companions...

Mr. Flowers looked into the face of each child in the rum shop. "Now, when you mooma tell you not to do somet'ing, all you t'ink she stupid, stupid, and go you own way, *oui*? It not new, you understand. When I was a bwoy, when Mooma tell me no, I do it anyway and end up in trouble. What you t'ink gonna happen with dese English?"

Little Gemma giggled and opined that since the people involved were adults, they'd get away with whatever they decided to do. A chorus of dissenting childish voices answered that the tourists would end up being punished for disobedience.

Mr. Flowers grinned and sat back. "All you want de story to go on?"

"Yes, Lis Twa," the children piped...

"Oh, it's so good to see nature in the raw, at her best, as it were!" Lady Jane rhapsodized. "How lovely to be off the beaten track, away from the madding crowd!" She spied a fragile orchid in the bush, squatted to pick the bloom, and sniffed at it delightedly. When she discovered it had no perfume, she threw it on the ground and poked it to pieces with her cane.

"Jane, why did you destroy that blossom?" Pamela scolded. "For heaven's sake, leave something for someone else to enjoy."

"Oh, shut up. The damned thing is quite useless. It has no scent!"

"Jane, where is Percy?" Henry broke his long-suffering silence as he removed his dead pipe from his mouth and looked around, resembling, as much as anything else, a hatted owl. "I haven't seen or heard him for the last half hour or so."

Capricious Paradise

"Oh, damn Percy, Henry. You know how he is with his bloody camera. He's probably sitting in some mucky place photographing termites or some equally disgusting creatures. He can find us when he wishes. Onward, upward! We're almost at the top." Jane forged ahead, hacking triumphantly at the delicate fronds of the fern trees around her. Then she disappeared. "Ohhh, God!"

"Jane, what is it?" Pamela cried, alarmed. "Where are you?" She turned in a tight circle.

"I've fallen down a bloody hole! Come quickly. I've hurt my ankle."

They could hear her muffled voice somewhere ahead. Henry bumbled forward, searching the ground in front of him for the place Jane had fallen into. "Pamela," he said, "it looks as if it's going to rain any moment. We'll have to find shelter." His pipe dropped from his mouth and disappeared in the undergrowth. Henry went down on his knees. "Damn and blast, I'll never find it in all this bush!" He groped through the dank leaves that covered the ground, and the strange plants and insects that grew among the detritus. "Ah, here it is!" He raised his pipe triumphantly as he stood, then took another stumbling step through the heavy greenery. "Jane, call out again, will you? Your voice will guide us."

Lady Jane emitted a terrified scream. "Dear God, there's a spider down here with me—an enormous one! Do hurry!"

Henry lunged forward and almost fell into the crater with her. "There you are! Frightfully hard to see, this hole of yours. No wonder you dropped in. Jane, whatever are you screaming about? Here, give me your hand, and I'll lift you out." He stashed his pipe in a deep pocket, braced himself, winked at his wife, and leaned forward to grab Lady Jane's wrists. "Heave-ho!" His hands slipped, and Lady Jane plunged back into the pit.

Pamela looked on and struggled to appear appropriately concerned.

"Jane, you've got to clean the muck from your hands, else I can't hold you," Henry said.

"Henry, you're an idiot! Arrrhhh! It's moving toward me! Pamela, stop peering at me like some fool and help Henry!"

The two of them knelt in the undergrowth and took hold of Lady Jane's wrists. At a signal from Henry, Pamela jerked ineffectively, lost her grip, and fell to one side, then rolled downhill a few feet. Lady Jane almost succeeded in pulling Henry into the pit with her.

"Stand up, you cretins! How can you hope to remove me from this place when you're kneeling? You need leverage, Henry, leverage. Where's your brain?"

"And you, Jane, need to lose a few stone," Henry retorted, stung. "Once more, Pamela." His wife struggled to her feet and again took one of Jane's wrists. "Heave-ho!"

Lady Jane scrabbled her feet frantically against the muddy walls of her prison, crushed the spider, and came clear. Henry dumped her unceremoniously onto the forest floor, then wiped his hands on a handkerchief. "Good show, what?"

"You might have been quicker, Henry, and more careful. I have injured my ankle, I told you. Suppose that horrible spider had been poisonous? And," she said pointedly, "I am not overweight!" Lady Jane glared at him, then tenderly examined her lower leg, which was already very swollen. She removed her hiking boot and gasped with pain. "You two will have to carry me until we can find Percy."

"Oh, Jane, we shall have to clean you up a bit, what? You're all twiggy!" Pamela, stifling a braying giggle, went to Jane and brushed awkwardly at the mud and leaves stuck to her clothes.

"For God's sake, stop pawing me! I am perfectly capable of brushing myself down. Give me your arm." She clawed and yanked at their clothing for support, hauled herself erect, hobbled a few feet from the hole, then sat down again. "You would think they'd have the intelligence to mark cavities like that! I shall lodge a very strong complaint with the Society." She rubbed her ankle, then rose again, hanging on to her companions. "We've only a few feet more to the top of the mountain, and reach it we will." She pushed her discarded boot into Pamela's hands. "Consider this our very own Everest!

Tallyho!" Clinging like some misshapen liana to Henry, she urged her companions upward, hopping on her good foot while Henry half carried her through the undergrowth.

"Jane," Henry reminded, casting a worried look at the black and lowering sky, "where is Percy?"

"Who cares? He'll find us. Shout for him."

At that moment the heavens opened. In seconds the threesome were drenched; their clothing plastered to their bodies. The ground became a slippery, sliding, mud-filled nightmare...

"Now," Mr. Flowers said, laughing, "all you know how de rain fall in de forest. It like a torrent from de sky, drops big like *crapaud*, and when dey fall, you can't see in front you face."

"Where Sir Percy?" Gemma asked.

"He down de hill, taking picture," another child explained.

"When dey find de lizard, Lis Twa?"

"What gonna happen to dem, Lis Twa?"

"You see," the old man promised. "You see..."

Unamused by the cooling shower, Jane bellowed into Henry's ear, "We've got to find shelter! With my ankle like this, I cannot go on in this damnable mud. Let Pamela help me, and you go find us some bloody shelter! Do I have to think of everything?"

"Right-o!" he yelled back. Cheerfully, Henry let Lady Jane slump into his wife's arms and forged ahead. After a few feet he peered blindly back toward them over his shoulder. "Follow me!"

Henry stepped into a bare, muddy spot and plunged sideways, sliding downhill some thirty feet. He rose, gooey, and squinted through the downpour, then fell again when the women, who had slid after him, brought up sharply at his feet, slathered from head to foot with muck.

Lady Jane howled with pain. "Damn you, Henry, you're an incompetent! Look at me!"

Henry looked at her and laughed shortly. She resembled a chocolate-covered Pekinese. "I can't see a foot in front of my face, Jane. Be patient." The rain stung his tender skin like a thousand bees. "If you'll just be quiet for a moment, I shall carry on!" He stumbled forward. The downpour let up for a moment. "I think I see a cavern just ahead of us."

The air was split with a barbaric sound. *Ekekekeekekekekek ekekekekek*!

"What in heaven's name was that noise?" Pamela yowled, shaking with sudden fright.

"How the hell should I know?" Henry shouted. "Come, there's a cave." He backtracked down the hill, took Lady Jane's other arm, then hauled her forward and upward.

The grotto was dank. They stumbled over and between giant stalagmites to get in, but it was quite cozy compared to the torrent falling outside. Unfortunately, the air around them held a rather unpleasant odor; one could almost describe it as halitosis.

"I say, Henry," Lady Jane complained, "your cave has bad breath!"

A strong wind blew in and out of the cave at intervals, whistling eerily, as regular as breathing. The ground was strange looking; it was pebbly in texture, very rough in the center but smoothing toward the sides. There were ridges and overlaps. In the back of the cave could be seen what appeared to be a portal.

Pamela helped Lady Jane sink down with a sigh of relief on a smaller stalagmite. Meanwhile, Henry looked about him, wiping water from his eyes. The roof of the cave had a vaulted appearance, quite nice, he thought, but a strange color--a rather orangy yellowy red. The stalagmites and stalactites were most peculiarly placed, all around the entrance of the cave but nowhere else. They almost looked like teeth, he realized, a double row of them. He snickered at his vivid imagination.

Lady Jane looked around and listened intently. "Do you hear that drum? It's quite a rapid beat. Do you suppose the natives have discovered we're lost and are using bush telegraph?"

"Jane, we are in St. Lucia, not Africa," Henry explained with labored patience as he began to make his way farther into the cave.

Capricious Paradise

"Henry, darling, where are you going?" Pamela called over the roar of the rain outside. "And what is this wind? It keeps going back and forth and is quite strong." She stumbled as a particularly heavy gust blew inward.

"Exploring. I want to see what's behind this wall."

"Don't be a fool, Henry," Lady Jane cried fretfully. "Come and make a little fire so we can dry off a bit. I certainly don't intend catching pneumonia so you can play Boy Guides. Come back at once!" She winced. "My ankle is aching from the chill."

Henry stumbled back toward them. The ground was moving slightly, quivering. "I say, do you think we're having an earthquake? I distinctly felt the ground shake!"

"Oh, I do hope not!" his wife moaned. Then she gasped. "Henry, what if we should be caught in a mud slide?"

"Don't be silly, Pamela! We're inside a cave. We can hardly get caught in a mud slide!" Lady Jane moved uneasily as another tremor shook them.

A strange noise surrounded them---*rummmmph*!---then they were inundated by air so foul Henry thought he might faint.

"Dear God, what is that smell?" Jane asked. "Henry, is something dead back there?"

Henry came back to Lady Jane. "I don't see anything, but God, it stinks! How the devil am I supposed to build a fire from wet wood?" He was annoyed.

"Oh, use your head! Look about you, at all that mossy stuff. Use it; some of it must be dry! Come, Henry, build a fire at once! I am shivering!"

Pamela and Henry gathered the mossy mess from about the stalagmites and piled it near Lady Jane. Henry pulled out his waterproof matches and wasted nearly half of them trying to light the stuff. He recoiled in disgust at its awful, nauseating odor. Only when the wind blew from the entrance of the cave were they spared the awful stink. At last the flames rose, and the little fire began to give off a most comforting heat.

"Ah, that's more like it," Lady Jane remarked nasally. She settled more comfortably on her stalagmite. She was holding her nose, and the others did the same. "Nothing like roughing it, what? Now, if we only had a spot of brandy and some bandage, we'd be quite well-off."

Ekekekekekekekeke ekekekekekek! Suddenly they were tumbled from their seats and rolled about between the stalagmites. The three of them fought to regain their footing in the upheaval...

Mr. Flowers's eyes were solemn as he gazed at the children. "Bwoy, de lizard really vex! Dem English build a fire in he mouth and it burning he tongue! It like he drink up a gallon of pepper sauce, and de inside hot, hot! So he go chomp, chomp, chomp, and feel somet'ing nice and tasty in de mouth, and he swallow! And what you t'ink happen?"

"What, Lis Twa?" one of the little boys asked.

"De lizard slither off in de rain, back to de top of Mount Gimi, water running off de leathery hide like a river—and dat was de end of Lady Jane and she friends."

"Bwoy, Lis Twa," little Gemma remarked, "me mooma tell we about dat lizard, but me t'ink she making up a story!" Her eyes were huge in her face.

"Why you t'ink she don't want you running off into de forest, Gemma? It so de lizard can't get you and eat you, like he did Lady Jane." The old man nudged Charlie and inclined his head toward Miss Lucy, who was grinning broadly. His tale had changed her mood, just as he had intended. "See? We did de English back."

"What happen with Sir Percy, Lis Twa?" came another little voice.

"He live happy ever after because he don't have no woman yowling in he ear like mad cat, dat's what."

"A lucky mon," one of the farmers remarked.

"Amen!" the drinkers chorused as Miss Lucy poured another round.

"Bwoy, Sir Percy brave to find he way on he ownsome back to de trail," one of the little boys piped.

"He ain't so brave, chile," the old man replied. "When next I tell a story, I tell you about someone really brave..."

TIKI

It was a Saturday afternoon. Charlie Prudhomme had put in a hard day's work. He stopped by Miss Lucy's rum shop for a toddy, as was his custom, before heading homeward.

None of the bar regulars was there except for Mr. Flowers. They greeted each other, friends now, had a quiet drink, then settled down comfortably for a chat.

"Bwoy, de place quiet, quiet," the elderly man remarked.

"Well, everyone has gone to Castries for their shopping," Charlie reminded him.

"Yeah, you right, but de children be here soon." The old storyteller sat in his chair. "You know, *garçon*, I vex."

"What vexes you, sir?" Charlie asked.

"Life ain't fair, dat what vex me. I get a letter from a friend in Carriacou last week, and he tell me about he part in de big war in Grenada and how he ain't even get a thanks from de Americans."

Miss Lucy waited on a customer, then joined them. Grinning, she leaned against the counter. "Lis Twa, you haven't been near a post office in years. How you get the letter?"

"My cousin Twilla from Carriacou fly up on de small plane. She bring me de letter and a cake fulla dat good Grenada chocolate."

"Are you getting ready to tell another story, Lis Twa?" Miss Lucy wanted to know.

"Well, I can tell you about Tiki if you want to hear about him. He de one who send me de letter, and it full of all kind of excitement." He hesitated, looking around at the almost empty rum shop, then shrugged. Normally he had a large audience.

"If you insist, I tell you about Tiki."

"Oh, God, Lis Twa, get on with it!" she urged, laughing.

He grinned delightedly as two children came through the door. They smiled shyly and sat down. "All you just in time for a story. Tiki is dis tiny, tiny little fella in Carriacou. Now you know dat de island just north of Grenada, and it part of Grenada. De rest of de Grenadines belong to St. Vincent.

"Bwoy, when Gairy de prime minister in Grenada, he don't like Carriacou. All dem vote against him, and he hate dem good. He don't even give dem school or road. Gairy was a scamp, *oui?*

"You know dem people on Petite Martinique, right next to Carriacou? Well, Gairy hate dem so bad he don't even give dem electricity, and dey had to wait until Maurice Bishop become prime minister to get light on de island.

"Well, Tiki grew up in Carriacou. He mooma poor, poor, and dey live in a little shack outside Hillsborough, which is de capital. I mean a *little* shack, only eight feet by ten feet, and it sit crooked on de ground and have pitchy patchy roof.

"Tiki mooma too poverty to send him to school, and dey don't have a lot to eat, so he tiny, tiny when he reach a mon."

With his two hands, Mr. Flowers indicated a man about five feet tall and then sketched in the air the frame of someone very thin.

"But Tiki smart, even though he didn't go to school, and he a good bwoy. From de time he six year, he help he mooma, working for de tourists, guiding dem around de island. A English lady teach him to read and write. And when he big enough to cotch fish, he work for a fishermon.

"Every day, rain or sun, dey take de boat, a long, skinny t'ing shape like a dugout, out around Carriacou, and throw in de line. Some days dey cotch barracuda; some days dey cotch arse..."

Tiki loved fishing. He liked the quiet of the water—when old Bajus shut his mouth; the elderly man talked far too much—when all he could hear were the rippling of the wavelets against the hull and the sigh of the breeze in his ear. And Tiki enjoyed the tension of the string in his hand, the fish at the other end, fighting for its life.

By the time Tiki was fourteen, he knew all about fighting for his life; he was one of the smallest people on Carriacou. The other boys taunted him about his size and beat him often.

"Eh-*eh*," Tiki would answer, "mon don't have to be tall or fat to be mon."

"Yeah, yeah, but bwoy, you smaller dan small," his tormenters would reply, laughing cruelly. "You *mawga!*"

Tiki paid them no mind. While the others lounged around the rum shop in Hillsborough, drinking beer or stout and ogling the young women who passed by, Tiki worked. He helped tend pigs, did his fishing, and cut bush. Unlike the other young men, Tiki saved his money.

When he was twenty, he had saved enough to buy his own fishing boat. This was the biggest moment in his life. The wooden craft was twenty feet long, three feet wide, and made of rough planks set with two strakes on either side of the bottom for stability. She was painted bright yellow and fitted with rowlocks and one seat. He looked at her and felt as if he were fifteen feet tall. It was his very own. *Tiki Own* was what he named her.

His mooma and Maji, his pretty, pretty little love, walked around the craft making admiring noises. They were both very impressed with Tiki's accomplishment.

From that time he was out on the water every day in the blessed quiet, fishing. Each morning he would leave his mother's shack at two-thirty, row out to areas where fish were most likely to be, and battle against them until three in the afternoon. Then, bone-weary, he rowed back to shore and sold his catch.

His mother almost burst with pride each day when she saw her undersized son trudging down the sandy path to the shack, a mess of fish in his coconut basket for fish tea, an island broth of whatever fish was caught, green banana, onion, and root vegetables, flavored with lime juice and hot peppers...

"Do you know de American lady live at Cap Estate in de north of de island, name of Jilly?" Mr. Flowers asked Miss Lucy and Charlie. "She and she husband have a yacht, but dey had another one den, name of *Tiki.*"

By this time another drinking customer, a farmer, arrived and became interested in the story. He picked up his glass and moved closer to Mr. Flowers and Charlie, who backed up a bit to make room for the man at the bar.

Mr. Flowers nodded pleasantly to the farmer and continued. "Miss Jilly tell me dat one day dey anchored off Carriacou, and dis tiny little fella swim alongside she boat and laugh. She ask him what funny, and he say she name de boat after him. Den Tiki introduce himself and dey become friend.

"She in Grenada during de big war dere, and she escape after de invasion begin. She say de bird save she, but I didn't know what she talking about. Dat another story." Mr. Flowers looked meaningfully at Charlie.

"Miss Lucy, I think it's time for a drink, don't you?" Charlie asked innocently. She nodded and poured Mr. Flowers a rum.

"I went to Grenada after de war, *garçon*, and de American putting in all kind of road and t'ing. Somehow Grenada ain't de same, you know? It become Mr. Reagan orphan, all mash up, mash up, like a unwanted chile." The old man shook his head and sipped his drink.

"Well, after Maurice Bishop and dem seize power from dat scamp Gairy, de island change for de good. It like all de little people, de ones out in de country, remember again dat it dey country, and it don't really belong to Gairy.

"Bwoy, if you see old woman fixing pavement out in de road, and people painting building and t'ing, and it really make you heart feel good because dey doing it because dey *want* to. And Bishop don't have to go out into de countryside to wash up in chicken blood and pretend he some big *shango* mon, because de people behind him.

"Life in Carriacou change as well. Cuban come and teach de fishermen how to cotch fish with fancy boat, special reel, and line. Bwoy, you shoulda seen de fish! But Tiki still go out in he own little boat every day and cotch a load of fish, and sometimes he make all dem in fancy boat look shamed because he bring in so much fish.

"Den change come in Grenada again. Bernard Coard vex because de people really love Maurice, but dey don't like him. So Coard try to mash up de show. He start playing cutie with de Russian, and dey move in.

"Bwoy, pretty soon all Carriacou run over with every bad john from Grenada, all dress up, dress up in military pant and t'ing, with gun and boot. It de People's Revolutionary Army—all de Grenadian who can't get a job join de PRA—and dey come to make sure de Carriacouans toe de line.

"You know how bad john is, nothing he do is right. He mash up what supposed to fix, eat up what supposed to save—bad john is a bad one through and through. It like dey raise in a cage and don't know how to behave when dey among people, you know? Mon, all de girl hide from dem..."

Tiki was almost thirty when things went bad in Grenada and Carriacou. He, like everyone else on the island, heard that Maurice Bishop was a traitor to his people. It was screamed at them from the radio every fifteen minutes. Then they were told that the Central Committee had arrested Bishop and taken him somewhere to teach him to be a good communist. No one had seen him in several weeks.

After Bishop's arrest, things got worse in Carriacou for the little people. They had never conformed to party policy; they didn't even know what it was. The soldiers of the PRA battered in doors, stole men from their shacks in the middle of the night and tortured or killed them for infractions of rules no one had heard of. Rape was an everyday horror for young girls and nubile women...

"Tiki in love with Maji, and he been saving up he money to build a house for dem. Maji tiny like him, like a bird, with a head of straight hair. I t'ink she have some coolie blood in she, because de hair so straight.

"He go to call on she one evening after he fished all day and find she all beat up and fulla bandage—beat up from de bad johns. And she tell him dey rape she. She all crying and shaking.

"Well, Tiki get vex. He vex more dan he ever vex in he life. He seeing red, and stars and arrows. It like he head on crooked or somet'ing. He heart pound and head ache like a bad tooth, you know?

"But what can one tiny mon do in a case like dat? He can't take on de PRA because dere too many of dem, so he decide he find some way to do dem back.

"Den dey hear dat America coming to invade Grenada because de medical student in danger. Eh-*eh,* Reagan a scamp, *oui?* All dem politician hang together like bat on limb. No American in danger in Grenada; de war dere between de left-hand politician and Maurice Bishop. But Gairy deposement now de excuse for Reagan. De elected official must be put back in power, dey say. Eh-eh, Gairy elect himself from de day he won de first election, and if nobody vote for him, he still win..."

Tiki began to plan his revenge on the soldiers in Carriacou. He started by ingratiating himself with the PRA soldiers, selling them fish cheaper than anyone else. It was rumored all over the island that the Americans were going to invade Grenada and take down Coard and his henchmen, including Hudson Austin, a retired jail guard who had been made a general by the Central Committee. Tiki believed the idle talk.

He started to hang about in the camps. The PRA officers paid no attention to the little man, but the soldiers noticed him.

"Bwoy, what you doing here?" one of them asked. "Ain't you suppose to be cotching fish?"

"Yeah, mon, but de fishing done for de day. All you expect me to work all night, too?" Tiki pretended indignation. "Why you teaching all de children to use dem nice communist t'ings like 'running capitalist cow,' but you don't try to teach me none?"

"Fishermon ain't suppose to be in politics," one of the soldiers said, sneering. "You job is to feed we."

"Mon, me hear on de radio dat Grenadian gonna get educate so we ain't stupid. You got to educate me, too." Tiki pointed to the man's gun. "What dis?"

"It a AK-47, mon. And if you not careful, I use it on you."

When Tiki left the camp that evening, he went to the shop that sold nautical charts and spent ninety of his hard-earned dollars for a chart of Carriacou.

"What de ass you want with a chart, Tiki?" the storekeeper asked. "Dat suppose to be for de tourist."

"Me want to mark where me cotch de most fish, sah," he answered cheerfully. "Dat way I can make more money. De Cuban say we must be scientific in de way we cotch fish, so I being scientific."

Tiki took the chart back to his mother's shack and put it on the wall. Carefully he marked the location of the big PRA camp east of Hillsborough and the others scattered about the island, then made some marks on it that would be incomprehensible to anyone but him.

After fishing all day, he sneaked through the dark nights to watch the camps and count the guns and soldiers. The information he gathered was put on the chart. When the big Russian ship came into the deep water off Cistern Point well after midnight, he watched from a hill as the PRA and the Russians unloaded a giant cannon. It went on his chart...

"You see how Tiki prepare for de Americans coming? All he have to do is take he boat and go to dem, give dem de information, den he do back de PRA for mashing up he woman.

"Tiki girlfriend getting better, but all de women on de island scared, scared. De PRA acting like a dog. House mash up. One old woman shot because she answer back to a officer. All dem who suppose to be *for* de people is *against* de people.

You ever see such? It like I always say, put a mon in a uniform, and he turn to instant jackass.

"Den de lash fall! Tiki wake up late one morning because de wind blowing like a beast and he can't go fishing. He go down to de rum shop to get a little bread for tea, and he hear de radio.

"Some woman screaming on de radio, 'De Americans are coming! De Americans are coming! Dey are invading we homeland! Go to you posts! Block all de road!'

"Everyone in de rum shop all excited and jumping up and down because war coming, and dey ain't never see a war. One old mon t'ink he gonna be on television!"

Mr. Flowers grew pensive, his eyes sad. "You ever t'ink a little island like Grenada be in a war? All de people see war on television, and dey know de blood ain't real because John Wayne in another movie de next week. Den dey find out de blood is real when de fighting start, and de hurt is bad when de lash fall. How a little island go to war?

"A mon in Grenada tell me, after de war, dat when de radio get on so, and de helicopter begin to come over de mountains, all de ole ladies run outside and get dey goat and chicken in dey house, like in a storm."

"They wouldn't know to do anything else, Lis Twa," Miss Lucy remarked.

"Dis friend in Grenada ask me, 'Who de enemy? De PRA is a bunch of bad johns, but dey is *Grenadians!* Who you fight, you cousin and he friend? And what you suppose to fight with, de goats in you yard? We like de Americans, so why dey invading we country?'

"Bwoy, de whole country confuse, and nobody know den how many Grenadian killed by General Austin and his men. But anyway, lemme finish telling you about Tiki..."

Tiki's time had come. He rushed out of the rum shop, his bread forgotten, and ran down the road. He could pretend to go fishing, then get away to help the Americans.

When he reached the beach, he stopped, confused, and looked around. His stomach fell to the bottom of his body and lay there, flopping like a dying fish. *Tiki Own* had been smashed. There were no other boats left, either. They were all piles of broken boards and splinters. A group of PRA soldiers were farther along, destroying the last of the fishing craft.

Tiki's heart constricted. "Oh, God, mon, what you doing?" he cried in distress. He went over to the remains of *Tiki Own*, staring down at his shattered dream, awkwardly patted the splintered boards to give them comfort. Suddenly he was blind; he could not see because of tears filling his eyes. He turned away from the soldiers, who were watching him, laughing at him, so they could not see him weep.

Head down, he tottered like an old, old man back to his mother's shack and sank to the ground. At last he recovered enough to sit on the step leading into the shack. All day he stared into space, paying no attention to the helicopters flying again and again over the island. He saw a white yacht sailing past below his house; his mind registered that it belonged to Miss Jilly, but he paid no heed.

Then, as darkness fell, rage began to build—a rage so intense that he thought it would make him burst, cause him to shatter like *Tiki Own*, and leave him a pitiful wreck upon the sand.

Tiki rose in the dusk and stood looking out toward Union Island, seven miles distant from the end of Carriacou. The helicopters had come from there, he thought, and he could not reach the Americans to help them. He was rigid with frustration.

A thought came unbidden, sneaking in like a thief, lurking, waiting to pounce. *You can swim.*

No, the rest of his mind told him, *you mad no ass! You get out dere in de dark water and you drown for sure. De current hard, hard. Or a shark get you. Den what you do?*

But you know where de current is bad, Tiki, and you know all de reef where you can rest, the other part of his head answered.

As if to emphasize the urgency, gunfire sounded in the hills behind his mother's shack. Tiki turned and went inside, then stood in front of his chart and studied it.

Gilliam Clarke

"What you doing, Tiki?" his mother asked.
"Me going to Union Island, Mooma," he answered in a determined voice.
"But dey mash up you boat."
"Me going to swim. I be all right, Mooma, if God spare…"

"Mon, you know what a swim dat is?" Mr. Flowers demanded of his audience. "Dat some bad water! Just off de northeastern tip of Carriacou is a set of reefs dat run over toward Petite Martinique. Dere is a tiny island called Little Tobago, and a bunch of rock, but de whole Atlantic come through dere. Den you have de shoals called Crablouse and Bedbug, and all kind of coral reef between Bedbug and Palm Island.

"Sailboat run aground in dat water! De shallow water bad enough, but de deep water is terrible. De current run like a young bull through dere." He paused and wiped his face with a tattered handkerchief. "Miss Lucy, I need a rum."

The woman poured a round, and Mr. Flowers drank his off in a gulp, chasing it with water as his listeners waited expectantly. "De night dark, dark, even when de moon shining, because when you in de water at night, it black like de pits in hell. In you head you see all kind of beast underneath you in de sea—shark, ray, octopus, monster, every sort of t'ing.

"Tiki sneak up to de end of de island, and when he see nobody, he ease into de sea…"

The night was pitchy black. The moon was to rise at about ten. The stars shed their pure light on the wave tops, giving the cold water luminosity and casting black shadows that looked like living creatures in the waves.

Tiki, dressed in a pair of ragged shorts, looked at the sky and shivered. "God, help me," he prayed.

The water, cold and unfriendly in the dark, crept up his thighs. His testicles shrank from the clammy chill and reached into his belly for warmth. By the time he was chest deep, he could not breathe. His heart's pounding shook his tiny frame.

Eh-eh, garçon, you scared of de sea? All you life you live on de water and in de water. Now you 'fraid because of de dark? Get moving, bwoy, and you be all right. Swim, or you be howling like ligaroo in de night.

Tiki took a sighting on a star, inhaled deeply, and struck out strongly for the shoal he knew was located only a mile or so distant. The direction in which he swam took him away from Union Island and toward Petit St. Vincent, but from the shoal he could cross to Bedbug and rest.

The current grabbed him and tried to carry him back to Carriacou. He fought doggedly, struggling in the sea, alternately spitting water and grinding his teeth, beating at the brine as if it were the enemy. A rogue wave smashed over his head and sent him under. He spiraled downward and came in contact with something moving icily beneath him.

Fear thundered in his chest. Fighting for life, he shot to the surface, afraid to look around, thinking he would see the fin of a giant shark. Sharks hunted the channels between the islands.

Eh-eh, bwoy, you swimming like a tourist! Why you fight de water so? It a friend, it a lover. Rest on de surface. Let it take you.

He continued on, but after an hour he was almost tired enough to give up and drown. The peace of death would be welcome. Then suddenly his feet touched bottom.

Shivering with cold, teeth chattering, he dragged himself up into the shallows on Crablouse. He rested on hands and knees until his breathing slowed. He struggled to his feet and stared across the worst part of the channel toward Bedbug.

In the distance the lights of Union Island twinkled, a beacon across the velvety black of the sea...

Miss Lucy, holding her breath, gazed raptly at Mr. Flowers.

Charlie exhaled slowly and smiled. "Quite a man, that Tiki."

"There is nothing on earth that could make me go into the sea at night, Mr. Flowers," Miss Lucy told him. "I don't even like going in during the daylight hours."

"All you West Indian women afraid of de water," he retorted. "You don't know how to swim?"

"No, I don't. I go for a sea bath each morning, but that's it for me." She wiped the counter and looked at him questioningly.

"No, I not ready for another rum," he replied. "Mon, de swim to Bedbug was somet'ing else, *oui?* De water deep, deep, and de current strong. Tiki, t'inking of he Maji, rest on de shoal for an hour, den he step into de sea again.

"De wind whipping up, like it do at night after de calm at dusk. It making de waves taller, harder to get over. Tiki swimming fast as he can because he so cold he feel like he gonna die. Teeth chatter like dey mash up in he head. He jaw ache from de cold, and once he bite tongue and taste blood. He can't spit because he know dere shark around, and de shark dey love blood. So Tiki swallow and keep on going.

"Den somet'ing brush he foot. He can't see around because de wave high, high, so he pray and keep on swimming. Den somet'ing else *lash* foot, and he draw up in de water, into a tiny ball. He bottom get a lash, and den he realize he in de reef off Bedbug. He almost cry he so glad de coral strike him.

"So he crawl out de sea, lie on de sand on Bedbug, with de one little palm tree waving over he head like a flag, and rest…"

The wind was rising. It blew over the small atoll, carrying the smell of the deep—bitter, chill, and threatening.

Tiki was racked with shivering tremors and almost too cold to move. He had no fat to keep him warm. His bones felt frozen. The beach still retained some warmth from the hot sun of the day, and that was a blessing. He tiredly covered himself with the tepid sand and lay, panting, until the sand began to cool.

The moon rose, a great orange melon in the inky sky. Clouds raced across its face and obliterated the light.

God, help me.

Tiki rose to his feet and brushed at the clinging grains of sand, then set his mouth and walked into the sea again, on the other side of Bedbug. This would be the hardest part, for there were no reefs on which to rest between Bedbug and Palm Island.

As he began to swim, the tide pushed him quickly toward Union. He tried to angle toward Palm so he could rest once more before trying to swim the rough channel between Palm and Union islands. He floated, then swam, then floated again, trying to conserve what little remaining energy he had.

He was about a mile off Palm Island when his strength gave out. Tiki wanted to live, had to live, but he had no reserves left. His stomach cramped from cold and hunger. His skin was shriveled, pruned and soft, too waterlogged to feel like skin.

He sank under the surface.

Tiki saw his mother's face before him, her eyes streaming as she prayed for his life. He saw Maji, his little love, trembling like a tiny bird as she strove to give him the will to go on. The scornful, sneering faces of the bad johns in the PRA mocked at him, their jeering voices echoing in the soundless dark of deep water. *Eh-eh, little bwoy, you too mawga to live, oui?*

He tried to reach the surface but could not.

Something hit his head. He put out an arm to fend off whatever had come for him, and his fingertips touched a wooden pole.

"*Eh-eh,* bwoy, what de ass you doing in de water dis time of night? You boat sink or what?" A fisherman leaned over the side and extended a hand to Tiki. "Bwoy, me thought you was a fish, me see de splashing in de water. And den I see de fish have finger. Give me de hand, and I pull you aboard."

The first hint of dawn had yet to show itself in the east above the heaving sea. The little boat bobbed up and down, dipping its prow in the troughs of the waves like some serf doing homage to a great king...

"It was some Vincentian fishermon from Mayero dat save Tiki," Lis Twa explained. "He out on de deep reef trying he luck in de light of de moon. Bwoy, de little mon lucky, *oui?*

"Tiki too wore out to talk. He just slump in de boat and breathe hard, hard, trying to ease de cramp and get warm. De fishermon give him an old shirt for cover. But de wind still whipping through de night, and de shirt feel like a cobweb.

"Den de mon ask Tiki if he hungry. Well, you t'ink dat de first t'ing de mon ask, yes? He give Tiki a bit of bread and a little piece of cheese, which was all de food he had. Tiki try to stuff it down, but it stick in he throat. Even he throat cramp up.

"Den de fishermon smack he head. 'Me stupid, you know! You need a rum!' He reach in de boat bottom, bring out a petit quart, and hand it to Tiki. 'Drink dis, bwoy, and it make a live one out of you.'

"Tiki never drink, but dis night he take down de rum, and de warm run like a blessing all through he body. He cough and sputter some, but he get it down. Den he know he gonna make it…"

"I got to get to Union Island, brothermon," he told the fisherman. "I got to tell de Americans about all de soldiers on Carriacou."

"Eh-eh, dem American ain't listen to you, bwoy. Dey fly over Carriacou all day yesterday, and me hear tell dey don't find nothing dere. All dem big white mon, you know, dress up, dress up in uniform and t'ing. You ever t'ink you see such in dis Caribbean?" The fisherman scratched his head. "Me hear Grenada all mash up with bomb and missile. Plane flying like seabird over de islands. All dem helicopter running back and forth, *wok-wok-wok*, through de day. Besides, de American over on Palm Island. Dey set up camp dere, and de mon who own de place strutting around like a young cock, like he make de war on Grenada on he ownsome. De whole damn world gone mad. Ain't a fish I caught tonight, you know dat? All dem bomb and plane scare away de fish."

"Brothermon, I *must* get to Union Island. Me have a friend dere, a white lady name Jilly. I see she yacht pass. She can get me to de American." Tiki leaned forward, urgent.

"Well, I going in now anyways. I can go past Union if you want," the fisherman told him. "But it won't do you any good."

"Me gonna try," Tiki said…

Mr. Flowers sighed and looked at them. "De little mon brave, *oui?* I t'ink it de rum dat save he life."

Charlie nodded to Miss Lucy, and she refilled the old man's glass, then poured him more water. He showed his appreciation with his toothless smile, then sipped from the glass. After he put it down, he continued.

"Tiki get off at Union Island and go to where all de yacht anchor. Mon, if you see boat in Union! All de newspaper people dere, from everywhere. Dey have French television, English television, and some mon from de BBC—German dere, American, even Canada represent.

"All dem rich from Grenada who leave de island before de war begin growing like bush on de beach. Dey posing up for de television, telling how dey just escape with dey life, how de communists like mad dog. And de newsmon trying to get into Grenada, but de American ban it, so dey running around Union Island like a set of ant. One mon even taking television picture of banana, as if it a soldier. Well! . . ."

It seemed to Tiki as he made his way to where the yachts were anchored that every boat in St. Vincent and the Grenadines must be in Union Island. Packed in the large harbor, they were bobbing in unison as the waves washed over the reef in the high wind. The hollow clank and slap of halyards against masts filled the morning with atonal music composed by Chaos in 1983.

Tiki spotted Jilly's boat and hailed her. She and the crew, Alex, came ashore and were swarmed over by media people.

"Oh God, man," she told one newsman, "we just came in from the boat. We've been here all night. Leave us alone!"

She took Tiki and Alex up for breakfast at the Anchorage Hotel, then sat listening as Tiki explained why he was there in Union. "You mean you actually swam from Carriacou?" she asked, incredulous.

"Yeah, me swim. Bwoy, Miss Jilly, me didn't t'ink me was going to live."

"I guess not, Tiki. Look, the Americans told me yesterday when I got in that I was supposed to be 'debriefed' this morning.

The navy is sending a boat for me at eight o'clock. You come with me, and then you can tell the officer your story."

"You t'ink dey listen?"

"I'll make sure they do." She flexed her muscles in jest, and Tiki laughed for the first time since his boat had been destroyed.

When the sailor came for Miss Jilly he balked at taking Tiki with him. "I'm under orders, ma'am, to pick you up."

"He's going with me, sailor," Miss Jilly insisted.

Tiki and Miss Jilly reached the building where the naval officer was to interview her. Inside with him were two Germans who lived all year on a yacht at Palm Island. They were reputed to be CIA agents, but most Americans in the area discounted that rumor.

"Why did you bring a nigger with you?" one of them growled to Jilly.

Jilly lost her temper. "Who the ass do you think you are?" she shouted at the German. She crossed her arms and glared at the naval officer. "If you want me to tell you anything, you get rid of these clowns. This man swam all the way from Carriacou to give you information and this jackass calls him a nigger? . . ."

"Well, de naval officer get rid of de German, one time," Mr. Flowers, chuckling, told his audience. "Mon, when Miss Jilly lose she temper, she mouth run she.

"Den dey bring Tiki a chart of Carriacou, after de officer hear Miss Jilly, and he sit down and show de American where all de big cannon is, how many gun in dis camp, how many soldier.

"De naval officer tell Tiki dey fly over Carriacou de whole day yesterday and don't see nothing. Tiki explain dat all camouflage. So de officer take de chart, excuse himself, and go show de boss, who believe it and act. And de American go back over to Carriacou and clean out de island.

"Tiki a real hero, *oui*? But later, when de American doing some—me ain't know de word—paying back for de damage—

"

"Reparations," Charlie told him.

"Yeah, when de American doing de reparations, dey giving people money to rebuild house, fix fence, repair shack. Tiki try to get another boat from dem. He ask real polite, hoping. Dey ask if dey mash up he boat. He tell dem no, but—and dey tell him no. Dat what vex me. Life ain't fair. De little mon risk he life to help de American, and dey don't give him another boat. Now he tending pig again, cutting bush, and saving money for another *Tiki Own*. And he have to start all over saving for he house. After de swim, Maji t'ink he a little god. Tiki don't mind de hard work—he accustom. What really hurt he heart is dey don't even tell him thanks. *Eh-eh!*"

SMALL BUSINESS

The day was dark, with low scudding clouds over the mountaintops and higher valleys in the south of the island. Heavy rain had fallen steadily most of the time, drenching the Peace Corps volunteers, Charlie Prudhomme, and the others who attended Miss Katherine McCloud's funeral.

Miss Kat'rine, as she had been known to the locals, was a Scots lady who had moved to Soufriere some twenty years before. She had finally gone to meet her Maker, leaving a hole in the fabric of expatriate eccentrics.

She was most famous for her flower gardens and her one-woman war against a Lucian farmer who raised cattle but did not fence them properly. The livestock repeatedly devoured her careful landscaping. After taking the man to court and winning her case but never managing to collect damages from the scamp, Miss Katherine decided to apply biblical revenge to the situation. Whenever one of the man's cows nibbled one of her prized hibiscus bushes down to the ground, she destroyed the animal and hung the creature's tail upon her front gate, to announce to the world at large that she had won yet another battle against the man. Shopkeepers advised visitors searching for Miss Katherine's house to "look for de tail gate."

The local constabulary, afraid of her prowess with her crossbow and the farmer's reputation as a worker of black magic, wisely turned blind eyes to the encounters between the two antagonists and felt no small relief at word of her death from natural causes.

The mourners at Miss Katherine's funeral had almost drowned during the service; the orations and eulogies at graveside were incredibly long and wordy, as obstinate as the rain. Thoroughly bedraggled, Charlie and two of the Peace Corps people repaired to Miss Lucy's rum shop for a tot of rum to warm them.

When they arrived, Mr. Flowers was there, although it was very early for him to be abroad. The Americans were quite surprised to find him in his evening haunt, as his age was against his slogging through the mud that had been churned up during the downpour.

"Mr. Flowers, what are you doing out on such a day?" Charlie asked.

Lis Twa waved away Charlie's concern. "Bwoy, you look like you been to a funeral, all dress up. Who dead?" He settled himself against the bar and looked with hope at the Americans. "Mon, dis weather hard, eh?"

The engineer nodded. "Miss Lucy, would you pour Mr. Flowers a rum, please? I'm buying," Charlie offered.

Mr. Flowers grinned his toothless grin and looked Prudhomme up and down. "Where you been, *garçon,*—to Miss Kat'rine funeral?"

Charlie nodded.

"Who bury she?" the old man asked curiously.

"Snapp Funeral Home," Charlie answered.

"*Eh-eh,* bwoy, you see how it go? All dis modern t'ing messing up small business. It make Methodius feel bad when de family get Snapp or Ramphal to do de burying, and he don't get to rent out he handles."

"A pity, too," Miss Lucy added. "He's almost finished with his own coffin."

"What are you two talking about?" Charlie asked, nodding to Miss Lucy to refill Mr. Flowers's glass.

"It all start years ago," Mr. Flowers began, prompting the Americans to settle in, "when Methodius a small bwoy on de estate of Mr. Kindred..."

Gilliam Clarke

When Mr. Josephus Kindred had come out from England, he was most unwilling to take up residence at his son's plantation in St. Lucia. In his mind, he was moving to deepest, darkest nowhere, far from civilization and its accouterments.

Among his personal effects, he had brought a card table, for he loved bridge; a number of tins of Carr's Water Biscuits, which he preferred for his cheese; and a decent coffin. He had no intention of being buried in a box of pine or some dubious exotic wood when he passed on to his reward, however paltry that reward might be.

The coffin was a magnificent thing, of good English oak, heavily carved and highly polished, and possessed of a number of brass studs, handles, hinges, and such.

When the old man finally dropped dead of apoplexy while screaming at a servant who understood not a word of English, his relieved family placed him in his ornate coffin and prepared to bury him in the little graveyard at the plantation.

The entire staff of workers was ordered to attend the funeral, so that someone other than the immediate family might witness the rites. The old man had made no friends.

Methodius was an impressionable boy of fourteen at the time of the burial. He, like his father before him, worked on the estate cleaning bush, picking cacao, and tending and harvesting bananas. He was a large lad and quite bright but completely without education. The natives were kept in comfortable ignorance in those days. Education was considered a boon possible for only a few colonials.

As Methodius stood under a cacao tree and enjoyed the funereal spectacle, he was extremely impressed by the beautiful box in which the old man had been laid to rest. The polished wood gleamed in the brilliant sunlight, while the brass decorations flashed blindingly as the procession wound its way through the tropical undergrowth and overhanging cacao trees to the graveyard.

That night Methodius had a dream of his own burial, but he was laid to rest in the same sort of makeshift pine box in which every other St. Lucian was interred. Then, in the dream, the box changed, became a carved splendor made of mahogany with shining silver handles. He could see the faces of the mourners as they marveled over the magnificence of his burial chamber.

"Eh-eh," a mourner remarked, "you ever see coffin so? De mon was smart; he t'ink ahead."

From the next morning on, Methodius's coffin obsessed him. But estate workers were paid the equivalent of a dime a day for their labors, and every cent went toward the purchase of food and the few bits of clothing they owned...

"You see, Methodius begin to t'ink. He can't afford to buy no fancy coffin, and when you dead around here, you friend get together, buy a few pine board, and make a box quick, quick. Den you planted like a seed in de ground. If dey can't find no truck to take you to de cemetery, den dey take you on de back of dey shoulder, all walking in a row." The old man raised his empty glass and grinned expectantly at Charlie.

"Mr. Flowers," Charlie said, "I'm sure all this talking is making you thirsty." He nodded at Miss Lucy as he pointed toward Lis Twa's glass, then his own.

After Miss Lucy poured them a round, she leaned against the counter. "Aren't you going to tell about Methodius's business, Mr. Flowers? I think that's what you started off to do."

"Miss Lucy, if you ain't know de background, de story don't make no sense!" he fretted. "Right, *garçons*?"

"Right," the Americans agreed.

Outside, the rain began again to fall heavily, destroying what light was left in the day.

"When Methodius turn eighteen, he been working at de estate for almost seven year, and de big boss, Mr. Kindred son, Earl, give him a rise in pay. Methodius now making twenty penny a day, and he able to set some aside..."

By the time Methodius was twenty-five, he had saved thirty dollars. In the interim, he had gotten married and had two children to support, but he scraped together every cent he could, still determined to have the casket of his dream.

He went into Castries, to the small funeral parlor there, paid out his money, and returned home with a set of resplendent chrome-plated coffin handles. He was delighted that the first step had been taken. Next Methodius set about building a little chest for his treasured handles. He filched a piece of cloth from his wife's sewing box and carefully lined the crude box, then reverently placed the handles inside. After that, every week, he polished them lovingly.

But he was not satisfied with his skill at woodcraft. The box he made for the handles was sloppy, the workmanship poor. When it came time to begin building his coffin, which had to be perfect, Methodius knew the task was beyond him.

He went to Mr. Earl and asked to be put on as an apprentice carpenter at the estate. The plantation's woodworkers were in the midst of erecting several new buildings to house equipment.

"You've been a field-worker all your life, Methodius," Kindred replied. "I'd be wasting your time and talents."

"Please, sah, I must learn to carpenter. Just gimme a chance; I'll learn fast, fast, and won't waste no time at all."

In the end he persuaded Mr. Kindred and was put to work with hammer, wood, and nails. His fingers and thumbs suffered terribly, but he learned how to build a box big enough to house a tractor. Now all he had to do was scale down his knowledge a bit, to coffin size...

"Dat when Methodius become a carver," Mr. Flowers explained. "He learn how to carve flower and t'ing from de wood, and he begin to work on he first board."

"His first board?" Charlie queried.

"Yeah, he carve each board before he put de coffin together. It have all kind of animal hiding in de forest on dat board—*tattoo, manicou,* mongoose, snake—it even have a dog. And all dem mix up, mix up with flower and vine and t'ing."

"Sounds like an enterprising fellow," a Peace Corps volunteer murmured.

"Oh, yes, Methodius is a smart man," Miss Lucy agreed.

"But den t'ings get bad here on de island," Lis Twa said. "De cocoa market fall apart, and copra out of style or somet'ing, and Mr. Kindred estate start to lose money, so he lay off most of de workers and Methodius lose his job.

"By den Methodius have three board carve up, and he ain't have no money left for de food and other t'ing. He feeling down *down*, because each board for he coffin cost thirty-five dollar, but he ain't give up. Some of he friend suggest dat he use de carved board along with plain pine board, but Methodius ain't taking dat on. He wife go working for some foreigner cleaning house, but Methodius can't find no work..."

Tante Isabel, one of Methodius's neighbors, had died. She was over a hundred when she finally went to meet God and glad to be out of a life of semi-starvation and suffering.

Her family were grieving because they wanted to give the deserving old woman a grand funeral. But no such services were available in the south of the island, and the family was too poor to go to Snapp's Funeral Parlor in the north.

A pine box was duly built and the funeral procession almost ready to carry her to her grave when Bookee, her nephew, remembered Methodius's coffin handles.

"All you wait here," he ordered his family. "I be right back, and if I have my way, de old lady go out nice, nice."

Bookee ran down the path to Methodius's shack and greeted him, then explained that he wanted to rent the coffin handles for his aunt's burial.

"*Eh-eh*," Methodius answered, "dat sound fine, but how me get de handles back when dey buried with Tante Isabel?"

"You come to de funeral, Methodius, and take off de handles just before de box put in de ground. Dat way she carry in style to she grave, and you keep de handles for you coffin! I pay you five dollars for de rent."

Methodius thought that over. He needed four more boards to finish his casket; the rental money would go toward that end. The transaction made sense, so he went inside, lovingly removed his coffin handles from their box, took up a screwdriver, and went with Bookee to Tante Isabel's funeral...

"Dat when Methodius start he little business. After Tante Isabel bury, everybody talk about how grand de box look when de family taking she to she grave, how de handles shine like de sunlight. She sister, Simprina, say she even see Tante face in de handle, all happy about she funeral. Of course, Simprina always seeing t'ing—she tell me she see God in de tree outside she shack, so you know she ain't right in she head.

"But from den, everybody in Soufriere and around, even up to Victoria, want to be bury with Methodius's handle. Dat when two carpenter begin to attend funeral, one for each side de box, so de handle come off quick, quick, and nobody notice."

Miss Lucy poured the old man a rum, and it went straight down. The drink was on the house. She winked at him, and he winked back, then continued his story.

"Bwoy, if you see how business booming! First, Calixte Cazaubon die, and he family rent de handle. Den Eulemia Cadoo die, and she family rent de handle. Methodius doing better dan Mr. Earl Kindred at dis point, because de plantation really losing money!

"Mon, in three year Methodius rent out de handle twenty-four time! De coffin almost finish, and everybody in Soufriere dying to get to use de handle. Two Scots die and rent de handle, den one English, and even one American.

"De biggest funeral Methodius see to is de burial of Clovisia Delaide, because she come from a rich family, and dey want *aut'entic* Soufriere funeral. They have *four* carpenter, one for each end of de coffin, and one for each side! You ever hear such?

"Well, Methodius almost done with he own coffin—he have only one board left to carve. But Snapp mashing up he business, moving down to Soufriere with a *branch,* like funeral parlor some kind of tree. Now Snapp taking all de business, and you know what, *garçons?*" The old man was indignant.

"What?" the Americans asked dutifully.

"Dat damn Snapp take a piece offa Methodius. Snapp begin doing de same t'ing Methodius doing all dis time. When Snapp move down with he branch, he hear about *aut'entic* Soufriere funeral and de damn scamp Snapp now have carpenter going to funeral, and taking all de handle off de box dat de family buy—de coffin he import with de handles on already! He t'iefing de people money! Bwoy, what de ass he going do with all dem handle? You ever hear such? *Well!*"

A SPECIAL KIND OF HELL

They were alone in the rum shop—Miss Lucy, Mr. Flowers, and Charlie. There was a big cricket match in Soufriere that day. The team from the south of the island were pitted against men from the north—an annual civil war—and nearly everyone had left their homes to attend.

"Mr. Flowers," Charlie said, "don't you have a story for us? I know the children aren't here, but—"

"I tell you about Mad Ansel," the old man replied. "I don't like telling war story when de children around, you know, because children shouldn't know about war." The old man stopped and looked hard at Charlie. "Nobody should know about war, eh, garçon? De church tell we dat when we bad, we go to hell. But hell can't be no worse dan a war.

"Mad Ansel live in Belmont in Grenada. From de time he a bwoy, he strange, strange. He cotch bird, tear off de wing. He find a chile, give de chile a lash. One time dey cotch him with a machete. Dey say it look like he getting ready to chop a finger off one of he schoolmates. He mooma, Mattie, she try to explain he doing wrong, but he ain't take she on.

"He mooma real poverty. But Mattie a nice woman, and she try to keep de bwoy in hand. She take him to de doctor, and dat mon tell she dat Mad Ansel is simpothatch, or somet'ing like dat."

"I think she meant psychopath," Charlie explained to the old fellow. "That sounds like it."

54

"Yeah. Mattie don't hear so good. Anyway, Mad Ansel stay in trouble all he life. When he in school, he sent home for doing all kind of bad t'ing, and finally dey don't let him in school again. When he older he hop from one job to another because he just can't get on with anyone in de world except he mooma, and he adore she.

"De only time you ever see Mad Ansel's eye soft, soft, is when he look at he mooma. He go down de hill and bring Mattie water from standpipe; he climb coconut tree to get green nut for she. He even help when she go to de river to wash clothes; he sit on a rock in de hot sun and beat shirt in de water. When he don't have a job, he sneak in de night and t'ief *callaloo* from neighbor's garden for he mooma, den cotch coconut crab in de moonlight.

"By de time Mad Ansel twenty, he been in de lunatic asylum eight time. Dey say he rape a two year old baby; another time he nearly kill a mon for a piece of coconut."

"Good heavens!" Charlie exclaimed. "Why didn't the authorities put him away for good?"

"Eh-eh, *garçon,* little country don't have de money to support a bunch of crazies. Where dey get food to feed a bunch of crazies? You go into de asylum, and when you been dere a while, de doctor ask if you go out and behave, and you say yes. Dey let you go to make room for another.

"But when de People's Revolutionary Army formed, and Hudson Austin, de general, begin looking for soldier to do dirty work for Coard, Mad Ansel a natural, eh? And so he take de job. He get new clothes for de first time in he life and start to wear government boots. He given a gun, a AK-47, and de soldiers teach him how to shoot it. And he get money. It ain't much, but he can bring food home to he mooma..."

The day Prime Minister Maurice Bishop and his cabinet members were murdered, Mad Ansel was on duty at Fort Frederick. His commanding officer, Colonel Redman, didn't send him to the attack at Fort Rupert, for he had a special job for Mad Ansel—one that most Grenadians would have refused.

"What we have to do, Ansel," the officer explained, "is clean out de imperialist element from de lumpen proletariat. We gonna get rid of de chaff from de wheat, like de Bible say, and t'ing, because we must know who we can trust. Grenada must move forward ever, backward never, and t'ing."

Mad Ansel's eyes shone with fervor. "Yes, *sah!*"

"I making you a special force, Ansel. We gonna clear out all de men who support dat capitalist dog Bishop and keep all de men who for Coard. You understand?"

"Yes, *sah!*"

And so Mad Ansel was asked to step aside when the officer called together all the soldiers of the PRA in Fort Frederick.

"All you who for Bishop," Colonel Redman told the assembled troops, "get over on de left, and all you who for Coard, get to de right. All de patrolling you going to do is serious, and I don't want no politicking to take you mind off de work. When you on patrol, keep you heads on what you doing, understand? I ain't want no talking, chatting, liming. All you for Bishop are going to patrol in different trucks dan men for Coard, so we don't get no political arguments going when you suppose to be watching. Now move!"

Those in the army who were supporters of Bishop hesitantly separated from those who were followers of the Coard/Austin faction. The officer watched with satisfaction as more and more of the soldiers crossed to the group on the left. Most of them were very young men, still in their teens, with traces of tears on their cheeks from mourning their dead prime minister.

"Okay, dat all de Bishop people?" Colonel Redman asked.

"Yes, *sah,* we all here," one of the Bishop faction called. "What truck we suppose to get on, and where de guns?"

The officer did not answer. Instead he addressed the Coard supporters. "All you on de right, move off. Get in dat truck over dere." The troops shuffled across the compound and climbed into a large personnel transport. Automatic assault rifles were handed to the Coard men. Then, after a signal from the commanding officer, the heavy vehicle lumbered from Fort Frederick's gates. The transport's grinding gears made a grating sound when the driver shifted into low to get down the steep road.

"Now, Ansel," the officer said harshly, "I want you to execute all dem traitor standing dere. Shoot dem like de dogs dey are, one time."

Mad Ansel opened fire on the unarmed youths, and as the bright crimson blood of his countrymen spattered the building behind them, gouted into the clean air, and spilled on the dusty earth, he grinned. He listened carefully to the screams of the dying, so that he might mimic them later. Something in his mind began to hum…

"I never realized that the Coard faction had so many of the PRA killed," Charlie confessed.

"When I was dere after de war," Mr. Flowers explained, "some of my friend tell me about dat. Dey kill off about fifty soldier up in de fort dat afternoon."

"What a terrible thing to do!" Miss Lucy exclaimed. "Would you like a rum, Mr. Flowers?"

"No, Miss Lucy. Dis ain't a drinking story. It make me sick, sick. Some water would be nice." She nodded and obliged. "Anyway," he continued, "at nine o'clock dat evening, General Austin, who was a ex-jail guard, a real *iggorant* mon, announced to de people of Grenada dat de Revolutionary Military Council had been set up to run de country. He declare a four-day curfew and say dat anybody cotch in de streets gonna be shot…"

Back from the main road in Belmont, a group of elderly Grenadian ladies, including Mad Ansel's mother and her neighbors, stood talking before their tiny houses. Chickens pecked in the dirt at the women's feet, while two goats browsed among the greenery at the edge of the cleared, hard-packed yards and devoured whatever they considered edible.

Annie, Mattie's closest friend, finished chewing her final mouthful of bread and shook her head angrily. Several of their neighbors downhill had been taken away an hour before, one of them dead for resisting his arrest. "I don't know what de world coming to. You hear dat jackass Austin calling himself general and telling how we gonna get shot if we leave we house? If we ain't leave we house, how de hell we suppose to get food and water? No offense to Mad Ansel, Mattie, but I t'ink all dem soldier in de PRA real scamps!"

Ellie, Annie's first cousin, wiped her eyes and sniffed. "And dey kill we Maurice! Oh, God, what going happen to Grenada?" She had known Maurice Bishop since he was a toddler, as had most of the old ladies. Like them, she had been very fond of the man. Turning and staring at Mattie, Ellie raised her voice so Mattie could hear her. "What going happen, Mattie? Mad Ansel in de army now. Maybe he know."

"I don't know any more dan you do, Ellie, God's truth. I ain't see Ansel for days now." Mattie, concerned for her son's safety, uncomfortably shuffled her feet in the dust.

"I hear dey kill Unison Whiteman and a whole set of Maurice' friend," Annie continued.

"What for?" Mattie asked, bewildered.

"Me t'ink Coard want to become another little god!" Annie answered. "What de ass poor Renny ever do to get shot? All de mon want to know is why dey arrest him!

Now what he wife going do, with she all cripple up? *Eh-eh, breaking into people house and t'ing!*"

Ellie spat on the ground, disgusted. "Bwoy, ain't dat de way it go? Life too hard in de islands! Just when we get rid of one scamp, another come to take he place."

Mattie's interest in politics and the local killing paled before more immediate concerns. "I sorry for Maurice and dem, but how we going get water?"

In Belmont, everyone was hungry and thirsty. The people lived from hand-to-mouth, buying bread and cheese, sometimes a tin of sardines, as they got hungry. There was no food stored against emergencies or hard times. Their water was brought in buckets on their heads from the public standpipe on the main road, a hundred yards downhill from their homes.

Annie and Ellie, having no answer for Mattie, remained silent.

"Well, you see me?" Mattie said defiantly, "I ain't going go thirsty or hungry for no damned politician! Just let dem try to keep we off de streets. What we suppose to do, starve? Me only have two breads in de place." She angrily sucked her teeth and stamped back to her little house.

It was getting dark. Most of the ladies were afraid to leave their yards for fear of being shot. Armed patrols were everywhere, threatening. Mattie, however, with water pails in both hands, emerged from her little house moments later and started down the hill along the footpath leading to the main road.

"Oh, God, Mattie, where you going?" Ellie shouted so her friend could hear.

"Me going for water." Mattie stood proudly. "Ain't no damned soldier going make me go thirsty. Me *beau vex*, I tell you!"

"But de night fall, Mattie," Annie called. "Dey going shoot you, Mattie. It dangerous to go down dere now."

"Why dey shoot me? Me a Grenadian, just like dem. Me ain't involve in dis mess; I just hungry and thirsty, and me going for water. Besides, me a soldier's mooma. Dey ain't going shoot me." She trudged on down the hill in the deepening shadows...

"You could not have persuaded me to leave my house for anything," Miss Lucy said. "When you arm children—and that's what most of the soldiers were—you never know who's going to end up dead."

Charlie was upset. "I can't imagine giving guns to some of the riffraff who hang out in Castries, Mr. Flowers. You know the kind of fellows I mean, the street-corner types who stand around making smart remarks and playing young toughs like they see on television." He shuddered. "No one in the entire country would be safe."

"*Garçon,* you speaking de truth. Life too cheap down here, *oui*?" The old man took a swallow of water, then continued...

On the main road, a commandeered farm truck full of soldiers was traveling slowly. The troops were in high spirits, joking and yelling with one another, telling outrageous tales of their prowess with their newly acquired weapons, each trying to outdo the others.

"All you lie, all you. You ain't kill nobody," one of the soldiers taunted. "Me kill a mon last night. Me shoot him right in de face. Bwoy, when you shoot dem in de face, dey really look surprise, eh?"

"Me kill two up in Tempe," another boasted. "Dey argue with me about de new way, de *directional materialism*." He laughed raucously. "And JoJo, mon, he afraid, so he just shoot a chile." He patted his comrade on the shoulder, taking the sting from his words.

"Eh, Mad Ansel, you suppose to be so mean. How many you kill already?"

Mad Ansel grinned viciously, the memory of the blood he had shed that afternoon still humming in his brain.

"Mad Ansel only pick on chile and small animal, you know. You hear about de last time he put away? He cut a sheep, den skin it while it alive. Bwoy, if you hear de sheep bawl!"

The truck stopped. The sergeant, riding up front, jumped down from the cab and glared up at his troops. "All you suppose to be soldier, not gossip like a bunch of ole women. Ansel, you stay here in dis area and patrol. Anyone come on de road, shoot dem. De lumpen proletariat must learn to obey—dat what General Austin say. Grenadian going learn to follow order, or else."

Mad Ansel leapt from the back of the truck and waved his gun in the air. "Me patrol good, *sah*."

The sergeant re-joined the driver, and the truck rumbled off.

The quick Caribbean night had fallen. The stars, shy, peeked from behind the evening clouds blown by the trade winds. Mad Ansel strutted up and down, up and down the road, and hoped that someone would defy his authority. The killing of the afternoon had whetted an appetite in him, a yearning he had not known before.

He tensed. Ahead of him, in the dark, he heard a noise.

"Who dere?"

No answer.

He crept toward the sound. Someone was standing beside the standpipe and in violation of the curfew was filling water buckets. Ansel's bloodlust pounded in his ears. He ran forward. The humming in his brain became a roar as he raised his rifle. He saw it was a woman. That made no difference—she was breaking the new law! In a tattoo of gunfire he stitched the violator's back from buttocks to neck with bullets. As his victim fell, her water pails rolled and clattered on the macadam road.

Triumphant, Ansel ran up and knelt by the fallen figure. The roaring in his brain assured him that he had done the right thing. Her white hair was stained dark in the pale light of the stars. He could not identify whom he'd shot, so he struck a match and peered at her face.

His mother's dying eyes stared at him in perplexity.

"Ansel? . . ."

"Oh, God, Mooma! God, Mooma, me ain't mean to kill you, Mooma! Talk to me--speak with me, Mooma. Mooma?"

Her eyes dulled. She left him all alone.

He collapsed sobbing in the roadway. The humming in his brain stuttered, then ceased. He took his mother's hands—the same hands that had fed him, stroked him when he was a child, wiped away his tears. Now her hands were limp.

"Mooma? Mooma, why you in dis place? *God!*" His face wet with tears, his nose leaking, he stood and hurled the gun into the bush. He stared after it, his eyes drowned.

"Mooma?" He knelt jerkily, bereft, and gathered up the torn, bloody body. For a long time he stood cradling her and staring into the soft night sky. He watched the eternal stars, then he began to howl like a dog. His mad, stricken weeping filled the night and brought people from their homes to stare fearfully toward the road.

He could not stop...

"God, that's a terrible story, Mr. Flowers!" Charlie looked shaken. "What happened to Mad Ansel after that?"

"Dey say he put into de lunatic asylum dat same night, and he howl until he die two year later. Some guard feel sorry for he and leave a machete in de cell. Ansel finally stop he crying by chopping himself up. But you know, Charlie, de awful t'ing is what all dem damn politician do—how dey cause a mon to kill he own mother just because dey don't like de words another politician use. Dere must be a special kind of hell for dem, *oui?*"

"Yes, Mr. Flowers, a very special kind of hell."

MISS SALLY

Christmas was approaching. The rum shop was quiet during the early evenings, as all the neighborhood ladies spent their days in the capital bargain hunting, then caught the last minibus home. Their children were camped out with aunts or grandmothers, who kept them under tight rein.

Charlie Prudhomme was enjoying an unusually peaceful chat with Miss Lucy when Mr. Flowers hobbled in the door along with Gemma. The little girl exchanged greetings with the adults, then sat quietly, her dark eyes shining.

"Eh, *garçon,* I know I find you here. It cool outside, *oui?*"

"Yes, Mr. Flowers," Charlie replied. "Let me buy you a rum to warm your insides—an early holiday celebration. Gemma, would you like a juice?"

"Thank you, Mr. Charlie," the child answered.

"Eh-eh, dat a good idea. Thank you very much." The old man took his drink from Miss Lucy and downed it, then sat on the only chair. "You know, it so quiet it remind me of de grave, and dat remind me of a sad story."

"Have another drink, Mr. Flowers," Charlie offered.

"In a while. First I tell you about Miss Sally Perkins. It a funny little story, but a sad one, in a way." He turned to Gemma and asked, "You studying you English in school real good, chile?"

"Yes, *sah,* me study all de time. Mooma say she don't want me *iggorant.*"

"Eh-eh, you mooma smart. You know Miss Sally almost didn't make she own funeral because some stupid mon in Miami can't read English?"

"You mean Miss Sally who lived up in Belfond?" Miss Lucy asked.

"Yeah, de same woman." He turned to Charlie. "*Garçon,* she a sweet, sweet lady, Miss Sally. She poopa buy a plantation up in Belfond, on top de mountain dere, and she come out from England every year to walk in de bush with she spyglass.

"You know how English is about bird. Dey carry de binocular and sit in de bush for hour. Den, when de bird come, de English make all kind of noise about what kind he is, how many tail feather he have, whether he molting or fletching, and t'ing. Dem English crazy about bird.

"Well, Miss Sally look for bird, bush, and every kind of t'ing. She love dis island. Bwoy, she love it in truth.

"Den one day she poopa get some bad news. Miss Sally in England with some kind of cancer, and de doctors say dere ain't nothing dey can do to save she life. So Miss Sally come out here to die because she want to die in what she t'ink is paradise. Dat nice, eh?" The old man's eyes grew soft.

"It was a sad time," Miss Lucy agreed. "But is this the kind of story to tell Mr. Charlie and Gemma? This is the season for happy stories."

"Miss Lucy, you ain't know how de story end, so close de mouth! I have dat rum now, *garçon,*" he told Charlie. "Well, Miss Sally die, and she poopa have to send she body all de way to Miami, in America, because she want to be cremate. You know what cremate mean?"

They nodded, so he took a sip of his rum and continued.

"De funeral home up in Castries get de body all ready, and dey fly Miss Sally to Miami. De people up dere cremate she. Dey suppose to send she remains back here to St. Lucia, and she ashes gonna be cast in de rain forest, because she love it so.

"It was a terrible time for she mooma and poopa, because dey mourning one time. And den de bad news *lash* Mr. Perkins! Dey lost Miss Sally! . . ."

"What do you mean, they've lost the urn?" Mr. Perkins demanded into the telephone.

Mr. Snapp, the owner of the most successful funeral home in Castries, was beside himself. "Well, *sah,* I call dem about where is de ashes, because dey ain't on de plane, and I know you have de memorial service plan for tomorrow evening. De people in Miami say dey look into it, and den dey call me back and tell me dat some new clerk stick de lady in de parcel post, and it so near to Christmas!"

John Perkins sank onto a chair. His face was lined with grief.

"De people in Miami say dey have no idea where to look, or what to do," Mr. Snapp continued.

Mr. Perkins thought about the situation. Being so far away from Miami, he didn't know what he could do about locating the remains of his daughter. "Well, Mr. Snapp, just keep after them. Tell them to go to the postal authorities and make some effort."

"I tell you plain, Mr. Perkins," Mr. Snapp answered, "I don't t'ink dey doing anyt'ing—it against de law to send a person through de parcel post! You can imagine what happen if all kind of people sent through parcel post. De whole postal system would mash up."

John Perkins hung up the phone, praying, and buried his face in his hands...

"Bwoy, de word was out. Snapp Funeral Home lose a body! Everyone on de island want to know how Snapp lose Miss Sally and what he going do about it. One English lady vex so dat she cancel she arrangement with Snapp and go over to Ramphal's Funeral Parlor to plant she husband, and Ramphal only know how to bury coolie.

"If you see de whole island vex! You remember dat, Miss Lucy?"

"I certainly do," she responded, indignant. "And it was a disgrace. It wasn't the fault of poor old Snapp, though. He lost a lot of business because of the mistake made in Miami."

The old man's eyes twinkled. "Mon, when you lose business in a place small, small like dis, you bad off. Dere ain't dat many to die. But let me get on with de story.

"Miss Sally wake up in she urn, and she feel strange. She don't know where she is, but she do know two t'ing—she poopa and mooma grieving, and she gonna be late for appointment.

"She try to get up, and she rise out of de urn and look around. She in a room fill up with all kind of package, bag, parcel, all stack up, stack up on de floor. De wall all scar up, and de door some kind of dark gray metal, with a funny little window, like it have chicken wire in it.

"Miss Sally kinda drifting around de room, taking a look at where she is because she don't have any idea at all. She hear all kind of bustle and noise through de door and what sound like plane roaring in de distance, but she scared to go out dere. And she feeling funny, like she lost all she weight.

"Now, she know dat she lose a lot of weight, but dis is a *heaviless* feeling, like she made out of de air. She stretch out she arm and realize she can see de room through it, and it den dat Miss Sally know she a dead.

"She go back to she urn and sit down, t'inking hard. Now she know why she poopa grieving, and she t'ink she know what appointment she gonna be late for, because she tell she poopa dat she want memorial service and den have she ashes scatter in de rain forest. She really looking forward to being dere, with all dem bird and flower and bush."

"How sad!" Charlie remarked. "What a terrible thing to happen."

"Well, *garçon,* Miss Sally one smart woman, you know. She fix it in de end." Mr. Flowers looked at Gemma and winked. "Chile, you t'ink Miss Sally gonna fix it?"

"Yes, Lis Twa," the child answered confidently, her faith in Mr. Flowers strong.

Charlie nodded to Miss Lucy; she poured the old man another rum.

"Well, while Miss Sally sitting dere on she urn t'inking, de door open, slow, slow, and a mon she t'ink she see before in St. Lucia peer all shifty sneaky into de room. She say hello and how is he, but of course, he don't hear nothing. He look over he shoulder, den come into de room quick, quick, and shut de door..."

She realized then that he was a thief. She watched him from the urn as he began sorting through the smaller packages on the floor, pinching them, squeezing them. He would take up a parcel, shake it, and try to judge from its shape, weight, and sound the value of the item inside. He chose only small packages, things he could fit into the valise he had brought with him into the room.

Finally his case was full. He stood up and gazed about the place. His face was sad as he thought about all the valuables he was forced to leave behind. Then he froze at the sound of approaching footsteps and voices. Sally could hear them too.

The thief grabbed his bag and hurried over toward Sally's urn. He piled up several larger boxes and, barely breathing, crouched behind them.

The door with the chicken-wire glass swung open, revealing two men dressed in coveralls. They chatted noisily in colloquial Spanish as they sorted through an enormous pile of large, cotton duck mailbags, chose four, then left the room.

The thief, sighing with relief, stood and began to move away from Sally.

She was desperate. If he stole her, she could get back to St. Lucia and possibly be on time for her memorial service. She concentrated on gaining the thief's attention and called out to him over and over: "Please, turn around and take me! Hello! Mr. Thief, please turn around and look at me."

The man turned and gazed over the room once again, then went out the door. It swung shut behind him, emitting that particular disgusted hiss that heavy doors make.

"Mister Thief!" Sally screamed. She drifted over to the door and through it.

The thief was walking down the hall and whistling. No one else was about. He went into the men's room.

While Sally waited in the corridor for him, she could hear the roar of several planes warming up outside. Soon the man reappeared. "Mister Thief! Come back! You've forgotten something!" Desperate, she tugged at his arm.

The man stopped and looked around.

"Wait," he said to himself. "Didn't I see Mr. Perkins's name on dat package in de room?"

He turned and, with Sally at his shoulder, ran back into the mail room. He found the package containing her urn, bent over it, and traced the label with his finger. "Eh-eh, John Perkins, in care of Snapp Funeral Home, Castries, St. Lucia," the thief muttered.

"Pick me up!" Sally yelled into his ear.

The man scratched his head. "Well, well, what he doing importing t'ing into de country through Snapp? Bwoy, all dem foreigner t'ief. De mon rich, rich. He own dat plantation in Belfond and can pay customs. But he working some trick, and Mr. Snapp helping. Well, I t'ink I just help meself. Eh-eh."

He took a red marker from his pocket and crossed out John Perkins's name, then replaced it with his own. Sally sank back with relief into her urn. With the package in one hand and his valise in the other, the thief left the mail room and sauntered down the hall and into the giant terminal. Whistling happily, he went toward his gate to catch the plane...

"Bwoy, Miss Sally smart, *oui?*" the old man asked, chuckling.

"Yes, but how is he going to get through customs with all the packages he stole?" Miss Lucy demanded. She frowned at her old friend. "Mr. Flowers, sometimes you talk yourself out on a limb, you know."

"Miss Lucy, when he go to de men's room, he mash up de parcels, find out what in dem, den take only what he want. But he don't have time to open Miss Sally, so he take she to de plane in she box. Is *den* dat he run into trouble."

Miss Lucy subsided and leaned again on the bar...

The airline check-in clerk stopped the thief at the gate. "I'm sorry, sir, but you may take aboard only hand luggage that will fit under the seat. That box won't fit, so we'll have to check it." She was polite but firm.

"What you mean, I can't take it on board?" the thief demanded. "It valuable, and t'ing, and I must have it by me hand."

"Sorry, sir, but the regulations are clear. That box must be checked through."

"Woman, what de ass you do if it get lost?" the thief yelled. "You know what in here? I sue de airline!"

"Sir, give me the box, and I promise you I'll take it to the luggage trolley myself. But you may not take it on the plane!"

"Bwoy, all you American somet'ing else, yes?" The thief's voice was rising. "T'ink you order de whole damn world around. You know how many time I fly in you plane? You want to lose a good customer? I gonna report you! I never see such!"

"Sir, the box." The woman's eyes now held a steely glint.

With bad grace the thief handed Miss Sally over to the woman, then stamped away, fuming, through the gate. Several minutes after he had found his seat and thrown himself into it, the flight attendant approached him and held out the baggage claim check.

"Here you are, sir. You can claim your belongings when we arrive in St. Lucia. And be sure you do, because we wouldn't want you to lose this box, sir," she added sweetly.

Glaring past her as though she didn't exist, he took the ticket and stuffed it into his pocket. The attendant left him alone. He tapped his feet impatiently, and when the woman returned, lit a cigarette and blew smoke in her face.

"Sir, you're not allowed to smoke on the plane. Extinguish your cigarette, please."

The thief, again looking past the woman, frowned and put out his cigarette...

"Bwoy, Miss Sally *makko* every little t'ing because when she alive, she always want to go to Miami. She come out she urn and sit on top de luggage trolley. But all she see is de cloudy sky over she, and de bottom of all dem plane when she wheeled out to be put aboard. De poor woman never see much of Miami at all, eh?"

Miss Lucy, shaking her head indulgently, poured the old man another rum and handed it to him. "You do go on, Mr. Flowers, I swear."

"What do you suppose she was at that point, Mr. Flowers?" Charlie asked. "A ghost?"

"No, mon, she just heaviless. She spirit still dere with she ashes. A ghost, what we call *duppie* here in de islands, ain't still with he remains."

"I thought a duppie was called a *jumbie*" Charlie said.

"No, mon, duppie just called jumbie in St. Vincent and Grenada. Here in St. Lucia jumbie mean a walking dead."

Charlie laughed. "No, Lis Twa, a walking dead is called a zombie. They come from Haiti."

The old man slapped his knee and chuckled. "You see how stupid dem Haitian is? Everyone know a jumbie is a jumbie, not a zombie."

"Oh," Charlie replied. "Then what's a zombie?"

"Me ain't know, but let me get back to Miss Sally before she fly away." The old man turned imperious, as he did when stumped, and they quieted. "Well, is when Miss Sally reach St. Lucia dat de fun begin..."

John Perkins and his wife, Josephine, stood anxiously to one side of the baggage claim area as the luggage came through on the conveyor belt. They had met every plane that day, but this one was from Miami. Finally boxes began to appear. John and his wife stepped forward, looking intently at the address labels on each package, and praying their daughter's remains would be there. Her memorial service was scheduled to begin in less than two hours.

The Perkinses had discussed the problem with friends, who all advised them to hold the service regardless of whether Sally was in attendance. While John and Josephine were at the airport, their friends had spent the entire day at the little Episcopal church, decorating it with banks of greenery and flowers.

"John! John, here it is!" Josephine cried, taking up Miss Sally. She looked confused. "She's here, darling, but addressed

Capricious Paradise

to someone else. Look, your name and Snapp's have been scratched through. Who is this person, Antoine St. Jean?"

Mr. Perkins, tears running down his cheeks, hurried to his wife and took the package in his hands. "Oh, thank God, thank God."

Nearby, a man searching frantically for a package ran up and down beside the conveyor belt. As Mr. Perkins and his wife glanced at him, he scratched his head, then turned and noticed their package. "Eh-eh, what all you doing with me parcel?" he demanded. He charged over and snatched the package from Mr. Perkins's hands.

"What do you mean, your parcel?" Josephine asked indignantly. "Are you Mr. St. Jean? I don't know how your name got on the package, but see here? It was originally addressed to my husband, and it's been marked through." She grabbed Miss Sally from the man and held tight.

"Gimme de box, woman," St. Jean cried. "Me carry dis box all de way from Miami. Me even get in fight with de airline because dey won't let me take de box on board. It got me name on it now. And you t'ink you gonna t'ief me box?"

A customs officer, watching the exchange, hurried over to where they were arguing. "What de trouble here?"

"Dis woman t'ief me package and say it belong to she husband, *sah*," the outraged St. Jean complained, snatching the box away.

"This was addressed to my husband, officer," Mrs. Perkins protested, straining to regain possession. "I don't know how this man got hold of it, but my husband's name--here, see for yourself—has been marked through. I demand that this package be opened by your superior, and we see what's inside. It's from Del Fuego Crematorium, and it contains the ashes of our daughter."

St. Jean paled, then surreptitiously crossed himself...

"Well, poor Miss Sally getting all shook up, shook up while dey snatching de package back and forth, and she get vex. 'Look at me!' she cry to de customs officer, but he ain't take she on.

"De customs man find he superior, and dey open de package. And what you t'ink dey find?" Mr. Flowers looked expectantly at each of them, daring them to guess.

"What?" Charlie, Miss Lucy, and Gemma cried out in unison.

"He find Miss Sally ashes!" the old man proclaimed. "And she get she service after all, den she thrown into de rain forest from a high hill. And now she happy flying back and forth with she bird and t'ing."

Charlie nodded to Miss Lucy to pour a round, then grinned. "That's a wonderful story, Lis Twa. But what happened to the thief?"

"Oh, when he realize he caught, he make all kind of noise about he don't recognize Mr. Perkins, and he come on de package in Miami airport and see it address to someone in St. Lucia, and he just trying to be a help. You know how t'ief get on. And Mr. Perkins say de mon a hero, and t'ing. But you know, *garon,* de really smart one in de whole bunch was Miss Sally."

"How so?" Charlie asked.

"She smart enough to find a Lucian t'ief to bring she home. If she ain't find a Lucian, she be dere still."

"Why do you say that?" Miss Lucy asked.

"De way I hear it, Miss Lucy, dere ain't no one left in de Miami airport who speak or read a word of English!"

"*Eh-ehhhh!*" Charlie said.

RAMKISSOON

It had been one of those incredibly hot days during the dry season when the sun beats down on your head like a sledgehammer and everything takes on a silver-beige sheen and glares like a furious woman.

Charlie and the two Peace Corps fellows were thirsty and repaired to Miss Lucy's rum shop after work as quickly as they could. Soon all of them were drinking from bottles of Icy or Coke, whatever came to hand. The men leaned on the counter or against the walls and stared dully at one another, just glad the sun was going down.

Charlie had decided to have a drink of something stronger when old Mr. Flowers came in. He wore his hat with the donkey ears, today bedecked with garlands of apricot bougainvillea. He hobbled with a walking stick, but his eyes were dancing like a young man's.

Miss Lucy grinned at him. "Good evening, Mr. Flowers. How are you today?"

"I fine, Miss Lucy, fine and dandy. But, *bon Dieu,* I dry!"

Charlie nodded to Miss Lucy.

"Very well, Lis Twa." Miss Lucy poured a shot of white rum and passed it to the old man, along with a glass of water.

Meanwhile they all settled down to enjoy Lis Twa's latest tale.

The old man downed his rum and chased it with the water, as he usually did, then looked at each of the foreigners and

Gilliam Clarke

winked. "Remember de customs mon who help de Perkinses get back Miss Sally from de t'ief? Well, when I was a young mon, I work for a time in Trinidad. Bwoy, in dose days Trinidad full of lace house—all you remember dose pretty, pretty house made with carved wood decorations on de porch, on de window, like lace? Well, all dem gone now.

"Dere was a little chap, just come to me shoulder, name Ramkissoon, who work at de customs where de *Federal Maple* and other ship come in. Ramkissoon was a real *moko!* Bwoy, no one come in through customs when Ram on duty don't catch he arse!

"Dey tell me dat Ramkissoon reared in a tiny shack with one room, back of where dey burn all de garbage. He have four brother and six sister, and dey poor, poor! He mooma clean house for some folk, and he poopa spend most days in de rum shop, drinking real cheap Trinidad rum.

"Ramkissoon false name is Nuthin'. He poopa name him so because Ramkissoon come from nothing, he ain't nothing, and he *iggorant! Bon Dieu,* if you see iggorant! *Garçon* can't argue with he father, so he grow up Nuthin' Ramkissoon."

"Lord, Mr. Flowers, just tell the story!" Miss Lucy urged, laughing. "Bwoy, how you can get on so?" She poured him another rum, which went straight down.

"Well, when Nuthin' grow up, he get a temporary job in a civil service office. Den, because he want a steady work, he study nights till dey make him a clerk. Den he decide he want a permanent civil service job with a uniform. He don't like police or soldier, so he decide he gonna be a customs mon. Dat when he work and study, and study and work. And what you t'ink happen? One day he actually get de job! *Bon Dieu,* if you see mon proud! If you see mon strutting! If you see how he tell all he friend dat he *officer.* Style? You ain't see style until Ramkissoon pass dat test."

The old man's eyes grew misty; he gazed at the ceiling thoughtfully. The adults waited patiently for him to go on, but the children who had come in to hear him began to fidget.

He glanced at the young ones and frowned. "All you pay attention, now. You know when you put a tea bag in a cup, when water add, de tea make instantly? De water get all brown, brown, and begin to smell like tea? De same t'ing happen to Ramkissoon! When he put de uniform on he body, he change into instant jackass!

"It a strange thing about men, you know. Put dem in a uniform, and dey all t'ink dey a little god, *oui? Eh-eh!...*"

Ramkissoon was sent for duty at the customs wharf, where all the schooners from the small islands came in. He enjoyed his power tremendously. For the first time in his life, he felt like a big shot. One day a poor old woman from Grenada caught his eagle eye; she had a box of avocados and soursops for her friends in Trinidad.

"What de ass you doing with all dis stuff, woman?" he demanded. "It confiscate! You smuggling foreign food into de country." Paying no attention to her protests, he snatched the boxes from her and set them aside to take home.

Then he went to work on her. "Untie all you bags, woman! Take everyt'ing out de bags. We ain't like smugglers here in Trinidad."

He spread out all her belongings on the counter, then picked up a pair of panties. "Eh-eh! What dis? Panty? Woman, how you wear such holey clothes? Eh?"

He waved a nightgown in the air before him and enjoyed the lady's discomfort. "And you sleep in dis? Cow shouldn't have to sleep in such poor t'ing!"

The woman burst into tears of mortification. Now Ramkissoon was satisfied.

"Pack up you t'ings, woman, and get out of my sight. Smuggling. Well!" He planted his hands on hips and glared as she hurriedly put her possessions back into order...

"What an awful thing to do!" Miss Lucy exclaimed. "Checking bags is one thing, but to embarrass someone like that!" She glanced meaningfully at the children. "I hope he learned his lesson, don't you, children?"

"Yes, Miss Lucy," they piped.

"The fellow was downright rude," snapped one of the Americans. "I would have demanded to see his superior!"

"Eh-eh," said a farmer from the end of the bar, "back in de old days, *garçon*, dey had manners. I ain't travel in a long time, but I hear de customs much worse now."

Mr. Flowers cleared his throat loudly, a signal that there had been enough audience participation. "Well, Ramkissoon transfer to Piarco, Trinidad's international airport, and den he t'ink he really gone to de top of de world. You couldn't speak to him no more.

"Well, one day dis big, *big* plane come in, and it have a set of men with suit and tie on it. Bwoy, everybody around Ramkissoon bustling and getting on. Den all de men in suit come to Ramkissoon counter to clear, like you must in customs hall. Dey stand dere. Dey wait in de line while Ramkissoon take ten box apart—box filled with Christmas toy, shirt, book, pillow, every kind of t'ing! Den de men wait while he take a lady apart. I mean, he have she handbag on de counter, he sniffing at cigarette, opening de powder box, checking on de lipstick like it hide diamond from Guyana! He even make she open she mouth to see if she carrying gold teeth! . . ."

"Excuse me, officer," said one of the well-dressed men from the large plane, "but we have people waiting for us." He attempted to show Ramkissoon a small document encased in leather. Ramkissoon drew back in anger. "You wait you turn, like everyone else!" he snapped. "You, woman dere, come up here and clear customs." He called a lady from the back of the line and carefully went through her things, taking as long as possible.

Finally he turned sneering to the men in suits. "You may clear customs now. Open de bag!"

The gentleman at the head of the group offered him another small document encased in leather.

Ramkissoon didn't even look at it. "I say open de bag, or you going to be in here all day! You t'ink you can come into we country with fine suit and t'ing and walk all over we?"

The gentleman sighed. "Where is your superior, officer?"

Capricious Paradise

"My superior gone for a rum. He on lunch break. And when he done with dat, he'll probably take tea break as well. You going to open de bag?"

The gentleman sighed again and opened his luggage. He stood quietly while Ramkissoon pulled out all his shirts, unfolded them, and shook them in the air. The traveler remained silent as his suits were removed, taken from the hangers, and spread on the counter. His socks and undershorts were waved about, displayed to the world. Ramkissoon began on the man's shaving bag.

"Now see here, officer, you've gone too far!"

Ramkissoon, glaring up at the gentleman, pulled out a toothbrush and inspected it. "I am de customs officer here, mon, and you must do as I say!"

"Young man, do you know who I am?" the gentleman finally demanded.

The men standing in line behind held their breath, not daring to move.

"You in de hands of Trinidad customs, dat's who you are," Ramkissoon retorted, "and I let you into my country when I damn ready. I am de customs officer, and I am de final word..."

"Who de mon, Lis Twa?" one of the children shouted. "Tell we who de mon!"

"Bwoy, if I de mon," another child cried out, "I lash Ramkissoon in de head, one time!"

Mr. Flowers laughed at their involvement. "Well, Ramkissoon get his comeuppance, *oui?* About den, he feel dis hard, hard tap on he shoulder, like de finger trying to go through de bone, and he swing around, ready to lash de tapper! . . ."

Ramkissoon gasped and went pale.

The premier, Dr. Eric Williams, with his hearing aid and sunglasses, tapped him again, even harder. "And just what do you think you're doing?" he demanded. "Report to your superior, *immediately.*" He called tersely to another customs man. "Repack this bag right now and make sure that everything is perfect."

Then he turned to the harassed traveler, Premier Norman Manley from Jamaica, and apologized about being late in meeting the plane. The traffic, he explained, had held him up.

"No, no, Dr. Williams, the plane was early," Premier Manley insisted.

They went on in that vein for some time because, being diplomats, they could be both in the right and in the wrong simultaneously.

As they were getting ready to leave the customs hall, Dr. Williams turned to the officers on duty and said scowling, "You are civil servants, and you will be *civil*. Moreover, I expect you to recognize other heads of government from now on, lest they think all Trinidadians are complete fools! . . ."

"Well, poor Ramkissoon demote one time! He not allowed to wear de uniform again, and dey move him to some bush office on a sugar estate, where he assistant to the officer in charge." Mr. Flowers snorted. "But you know customs officer? While Dr. Williams alive, butter can't melt in dey mouth, but when he die, *bon Dieu,* how t'ings change up! Dey all go back to being a Ramkissoon, one time." He bowed toward Miss Lucy, courteous. "I thank you for de rum, Miss Lucy."

"And we thank you for the story, Lis Twa," she replied formally, dropping the old man a curtsey.

"Ain't it time for Miss Jilly to come see we?" the old man asked Miss Lucy.

"Yes, she should be coming by soon."

The old man turned to Charlie. "When Miss Jilly come, I get she to tell you de story about how de bird save she," he whispered. "Den maybe you can explain it to me."

"Be glad to, Lis Twa," Charlie whispered back, "provided I understand it myself."

With a smile and another bow to his audience, Mr. Flowers went out the rum shop door and into the dusk. The evening breeze blew the bougainvillea on his hat, and the garland waved like a flag.

SAVED BY THE BIRD

As Charlie approached Miss Lucy's rum shop, he looked with surprise at the Honda parked in front. It was unusual to find a car there; all of Miss Lucy's customers were local residents who traveled on foot.

Mr. Flowers came to the door, glanced around impatiently, then spied Charlie and brightened. "Come, mon, I been waiting for you. Have a lady for you to meet." The old man sounded excited, so Charlie walked faster. Mr. Flowers came outside to greet him. "You remember dat lady I tell you about, Miss Jilly, who in Grenada during de war—de same lady who help Tiki?"

Charlie nodded and took Mr. Flowers's arm to lead him back inside.

"Well, she here, and she can tell de story. Den, when she gone, you can explain about de bird, okay?"

"Of course." The two of them went into the rum shop, which was relatively empty now in the middle of the afternoon. Miss Lucy was chatting with an attractive white woman in her fifties, who turned and smiled at Lis Twa.

"I thought you'd deserted us, Mr. Flowers."

"No, Miss Jilly. I want to present a friend, Mr. Charlie Prudhomme. He American too. He work on de Soufriere t'ing."

Jilly and Charlie shook hands, then compared notes on the States and how Charlie liked the Caribbean. Mr. Flowers fidgeted for a few moments, then interrupted them with his request.

"Miss Jilly, I want you to tell Charlie about how you saved by de bird from de Grenada war."

Jilly's blue eyes twinkled. "If I tell you the story, Lis Twa, are you going to buy me a rum?"

"Eh-*eh*, you trying to turn de t'ing around!" Mr. Flowers laughed, delighted. "Dat de way I earn *my* rum, Miss Jilly."

"Just teasing—but if you want to earn your rum, Lis Twa, then you must tell the story. You've heard it enough by now to know it."

"Okay, Miss Jilly," the old man agreed. "You buy de rum, and I tell de tale."

"Very well, Lis Twa, it's a deal." Jilly turned to Charlie. "Mr. Prudhomme, do you know anything about the Grenada invasion?"

"Only what I read in the papers in the States," Charlie answered.

"From what we could gather while listening to the rambling spite on the radio," Jilly explained, "the reason for Prime Minister Bishop's arrest and subsequent assassination by the PRA was his refusal to sign some papers that he believed would have made Grenada a virtual satellite of the Soviet Union."

"We never heard about any of that," Charlie said.

"But you must have heard about the schoolchildren."

"I want to start at dat part, Miss Jilly. You can butt in if I mash up de story, all right?"

Miss Lucy laughed and leaned on the counter. "Jilly, you might as well give up." She winked at Lis Twa. "Well, Mr. Flowers? We're waiting."

The old man took a deep breath. "De schoolchildren make up a plan to rescue Bishop because dey vex, vex with Coard. Not many of de Grenadian like Coard, de deputy prime minister—he t'ink he have too much brain. So on dat Wednesday de children gather in St. Georges. Dey carrying a set of poster, placard, and t'ing mark up to tell Coard to free de prime minister.

"Mon, if you see de children! Every one of dem bring a mooma or a poopa, because all de grown folk excited about what de *pickney* gonna do. Everybody walking around in de town, drinking soda pop, chatting up with dey friend—it like a carnival!

"Den a set of Cuban come in from de airport in de big transport, and all dem have placard, too. Some of de sign read 'Free Bishop!' and some say 'No Bishop, No Aeropuerto!' Whoever t'ink de Cuban would get into de act, eh?

"Den de children lead dey parents, and all dem march up de hill, shame de soldiers guarding de prime minister—and dey free Maurice Bishop! But den Bishop was murdered at Fort Rupert along with some of he cabinet ministers. De PRA kill Bishop, Unison Whiteman, Jacqueline Creft, and a whole set of people who with Maurice."

"Yes, we read about all that," Charlie broke in. "About the murders, I mean."

"Well, Miss Jilly living in Grenada on she and she husband's yacht, *Nannette,* down at Grenada Yacht Services in de lagoon. She dere with a set of foreign yachts and two charter boats. Den, on de Friday after de murders, General Hudson Austin let de other yachts go, and only a yacht from America on de dry dock and Miss Jilly's was left."

"Yes," Jilly agreed, "Bob, the owner of *La Cautiva,* and I stood like lost souls on the jetty. We cried and watched all our friends leave. It was so sad to see the yachts going from Grenada. I've never felt so lonely in my life."

"Eh-eh, Miss Jilly, who telling de story?" The old man paused expectantly, so Charlie ordered another rum. "Anyway, Miss Jilly husband was in Trinidad, where he director of some big United Nations office, and she on she ownsome in Grenada when de *cutlash* fall.

"On Sunday night she husband, Sil, call and tell she to leave. He hear de Americans gonna invade Grenada! And he tell she dat de weather was gonna be real bad, too. Everyt'ing happen at once, eh?"

"My husband wanted me to ask Alex, a Grenadian friend who was an expert sailor, to help me take *Nannette* out of

Grenada," Jilly explained to Charlie, "but I told Sil that I was out of money and food. I said I'd go to the bank on Monday and then try to get out first thing on Tuesday morning. General Austin had lifted the five-day curfew and ordered the country 'back to normal or else.' Normalcy was scheduled to begin at eight on Monday morning; so in spite of the problems I had no choice but to wait."

"Man, that's between a rock and a hard place," Charlie remarked. "Mr. Flowers, you need a rum?"

"No, not now, thanks. Anyway, one set of bad john begin to harass Miss Jilly. Dey come down de jetty to de boat, saying dey got to escape from Hudson Austin and t'ing. Dey want she to hide dem on *Nannette* and sneak dem from de country. It a plot, you know! Austin send dem down to try and talk Miss Jilly into breaking de law so dey can lock she up. But she know all dem, and she smart." The old man grinned at Jilly and winked. "She tell dem to go to de devil, one time! . . ."

Early on Monday afternoon, when Jilly and Bob returned from the bank and supermarket, she began to make *Nannette* ready for sailing. The wind was blowing about thirty knots already, and worse was forecast. She prayed that Donald, a good friend and the immigration officer at the lagoon, had been able to get word to Alex that she was sailing the next morning. There was no way she alone could take *Nannette* out in rough seas.

When the curfew was lifted for a few hours on the previous Friday so that Grenadians might stock up on food, Mike, one of the American medical students, had come to the lagoon to see Jilly. He asked if he, his girlfriend, and a couple of buddies could sail on *Nannette* when Jilly left the island. She agreed, telling Mike to bring their belongings down on Monday afternoon so they could leave first thing on Tuesday morning.

"It's a pity none of your friends are sailors," she told Mike.

"Yeah, we're all pretty worthless when it comes to seamanship," he said ruefully.

The trip to Union Island, the closest land belonging to a country other than Grenada, wasn't a long one—only about

Capricious Paradise

forty miles—but the route passed Kick 'em Jenny, between Grenada and Carriacou. Kick 'em Jenny was shown on the charts as Diamond Rock, where the Atlantic North Equatorial Current met the Guiana Current—each one going in a different direction—and the bottom dropped from two hundred fathoms to about a thousand fathoms like an undersea waterfall. Nearby was also an underwater volcano, which sometimes grumbled. When the wind was up, Kick 'em Jenny was a very frightening stretch of water, and Jilly didn't look forward to sailing past in bad weather.

At three in the afternoon on Monday, Alex turned up, ready to spend the night on *Nannette* and go with Jilly the next morning. He had left his mother and his newly finished house unguarded to aid his friend. Alex helped her rearrange things in the boat to make room for the medical students' belongings.

Then Mike and his group arrived. The political confusion in Grenada and the curfew had upset the students, even though none of them felt threatened. Jilly took their passports and made up the crew list, so the students could clear immigration and go into St. Vincent legally. Then Mike and the others left the lagoon to look for Dramamine and rum. Bob, seeing them leave the compound, went with them...

Lis Twa sipped from his glass of water, then set it back on the counter. "Jilly go along de dock to de customs and immigration office to clear with Donald before he go off duty at five," he explained. "She also want to tell she friend farewell, because she worried about Donald. He not a PRA mon, and he watched, watched by the PRA! When she pass de telephone booth, de phone ring. It she husband, saying she must leave, one time."

The old man laughed and clapped his hands together. "Miss Jilly did pull a trick on Hudson Austin, you know. When dey put a ban on all foreign telephone calls, she write a note to General Austin saying she a diplomat immunity, whatever dat is, because of she husband. She write General Austin all about de Geneva Convention, and she tell Austin she must be allowed to speak with de husband. But since Austin ain't know convention from cowpat, he say it okay for she husband to call, and he allow de calls through. Den Austin tell she dat every call be listened to. Eh-*eh!* You see how de mon a scamp? . . ."

Jilly leaned against the phone booth, sighing, and looked around the empty yacht basin. "I can't get clearance to go until tomorrow morning at six," she explained to her husband.

"The Americans are going to invade Grenada at first light in the morning."

"You're joking!"

"No, I am not," he said. "I want you out of that place! Call me when you reach Union. And, Jilly, for God's sake, don't do anything idiotic."

The operator listening to the call broke in, yelling, "All you talking stupid, mon! Get off de phone!"

The connection was cut, and Jilly went on to the immigration office. Donald stamped the passports and gave his friend the sailing documents, then she went back to *Nannette.* She was very angry about what her husband had told her. She sat on the dock, Alex by her side, staring at the peaceful scene around them. She wondered if Grenada was really going to be invaded by her country the following morning, or if it was just another rumor. It didn't make sense—there were no Americans in danger.

"I can't fathom Reagan's reasoning, Alex," she griped. "Reagan has done everything he could to kill Grenada economically because he didn't like Bishop's left-wing stance. But Reagan doesn't give a damn about any of the people here—Grenadian, American, or otherwise. He's using the American medical students as an excuse. I've come to the conclusion that because his presidency is coming to an end without there being a war, he's filled with regrets and intends to rectify the situation."

"What do you mean?" Alex asked.

"Think about it, man. Poor old Reagan can see himself riding off camera, Hollywood style, into the sunset—before he's had a chance to fire his gun. Now he's finally seen a target and is about to pull the trigger!" Her voice was bitter.

Alex rose to his feet. His face was serious. "I'm going back to the house and tell Mother that there might be an invasion, so she'll be prepared. Be back in an hour." He went briskly down the jetty.

Jilly sighed and continued to stare at the water and the palm-lined shore of the lagoon beyond. Her reverie was interrupted.

"Excuse me, are you Miss Jilly?"

She looked up over her shoulder and saw a man standing behind her. His face was pale, and his head covered by an enormous Rasta cap. His clothes were filthy and tattered. He seemed to be in a lot of pain. "Yes, what do you want?" Jilly asked.

"I'm Peter Lucas. Donald told me to find you. I have to get out of Grenada, and he says you're leaving in the morning. The PRA are after me. I've been hiding in the bush since Wednesday."

Jilly lost her temper. "Mr. Lucas, I will not take anyone out of this country illegally. You can go back to Mr. Coard, or General Austin, or whatever asshole sent you, and tell them so. And you can tell them as well to get off my back!" She looked closely at the man when he didn't turn to leave. He had tears in his eyes.

"Please, Miss Jilly, please. Here's my identification. Take it; go check with Donald. I'm Unison Whiteman's cousin, and I have to get out of here. The only way I can leave the country is by stowing away. Donald can't stamp my papers—he'd be crucified! I was up at Fort Rupert, and just before the firing started, Maurice and Unison told me to leave because they were all going to be killed. I was shot in the head as I tried to escape. There was blood all over my face, so the soldiers left me for dead, and when I regained consciousness, I managed to get away. Please, go ask Donald." He thrust the card into her hand...

Mr. Flowers looked grimly at Charlie and Miss Lucy. "De identification card say dat Peter Lucas was a immigration officer. Jilly know he face familiar, so she feel like de card real. But she still ain't sure. She go on *Nannette* and tell de chap to come on de boat while she check with Donald.

"Den Peter Lucas ask she where de knives kept. Bwoy, Miss Jilly ain't taking dat on. 'What you want a knife for?' she ask, she face all mash up in a frown. And he explain dat if he caught on she boat, he can tell de PRA he force she to hide him. Dat convince Miss Jilly a little. But she go down de dock to talk with Donald anyway.

"Bwoy, Donald shocked dat Peter down at de lagoon during de daylight. He explain to Jilly dat Peter de only man left alive who could tell what really happen at Fort Rupert when Bishop, Jacqueline Creft, and de others were massacred, and if he don't get medical attention for de head wound, he might get infection and die.

"And Miss Jilly make up she mind, one time! She tell Donald dat she taking Peter with she de next morning.

"Den Donald tell she, 'Jilly, I'd like you to help him, but if de PRA or Coard's *garçons* cotch him on you yacht, you dead and so is he. Dey shoot you like a dog; nothing could save you. Remember dat!'

"But now Miss Jilly vex, *vex!*" The old man laughed at the expression on Jilly's face. "You know how woman is—when she vex she mouth run she, eh?"

"That's true, Lis Twa. I was so damned mad with Coard, Austin, and the PRA by then—I'd have done anything to foul them up if given a chance. They had the whole country in a state of terror! What would you do if some goons took over St. Lucia and started killing innocent people?"

"I lash dem, one time!" Mr. Flowers said with relish. "One time!"

"Good thing the medical students didn't know of your little plans," Charlie said, laughing. "They might not have agreed to take the risk."

Jilly shrugged. "They were off hunting rum. Besides, Mike would have backed me up, which he did later when I told him about Peter."

"What did you do with the man?" Miss Lucy asked.

Mr. Flowers looked exasperated. Clearly, they had interrupted him once too often, so they quieted, and he went on with the story.

"When Miss Jilly get back to de boat, she realize dere was no place on *Nannette* for Peter to hide. So she dress him up in some of she husband's old clothes and give him a bucket of tools so he can pretend he a mechanic if any PRA question him. Jilly don't t'ink ahead—dat if de PRA see Peter, dey recognize him. Den she take him down de dock to where a Grenadian couple live as caretakers on a foreign yacht, and dey agree to hide Peter until de night fall.

"When Mike and de others get back to de boat, Jilly take Mike aside and explain de situation to him. Dey agree not to tell de others, but to let dem t'ink Peter was part of de crew..."

When dark fell, Alex and Peter returned to *Nannette*. Everyone made the best of the cramped quarters. After a restless night, Jilly gave up trying to sleep. She got dressed at three that morning, made a cup of coffee, and took it out to the cockpit. Every night since the massacre, small convoys of trucks filled with dead civilians had rumbled down the dark road that ran along the lagoon. Jilly wondered where the PRA dumped the bodies. She watched another five army trucks pass.

At about five o'clock, as dawn began to light the sky, she heard a low, droning noise. She couldn't identify it, although it brought to mind something from an old war movie; but that didn't make any sense. Mike came up on deck; and it was not long before Peter, who'd been sleeping in the virgin berth—the name given to a small berth above the main settee—joined them. They saw two enormous planes begin to circle over the Point Saline area. Now Jilly realized that the unidentified sound was the aircraft engines. As she, Peter, and Mike watched, figures began to drop out of the planes and drift silently toward the land.

Jilly told Mike to wake everyone and get them ready to sail. He reminded her that they could not leave before six, the time they were cleared to go out, then went to do as she had asked. Jilly, meanwhile, hunted in the locker for her American flag, which she tied on *Nannette's* backstay. She also made certain that the United Nations' burgee she flew was visible and in good shape. She told Peter to hide in the head if anyone came to the boat.

As the sun rose, they heard the sound of heavy guns firing over at Point Saline. All of them watched antiaircraft shells burst in the air as the PRA gunners tried to knock the big American planes out of the sky.

"You can tell that the Grenadians, and not the Cubans, are firing the guns, Jilly," Alex remarked, "because they keep shooting at where the plane was, not where it's going."

Mike laughed nervously. "Even my aim is better than that!"

Later, the Cubans were accused of leading the fighting against the Americans by Washington, but the Cubans had been ordered to defend themselves if attacked, and nothing more.

Alex went below and tuned in to Radio Free Grenada, which would come on the air at five-thirty.

As the morning got brighter, antiaircraft guns all around St. Georges began firing into the air indiscriminately. The noise was deafening. Panicked people around the lagoon ran from their houses, wondering what was happening.

The radio broadcaster added her voice to the rest of the confusion. She was screaming, "Grenadians, your country is being invaded! Grenadians, your country is being invaded! Block all the roads! All military personnel report immediately to your stations. Doctors and nurses report immediately to the hospital."

They watched an old woman across the lagoon begin herding her goats and chickens into her house, just as she would during a hurricane…

Mr. Flowers paused for breath, and Jilly ordered another rum for the storyteller. He nodded his thanks, took a sip, then continued. "Jilly tell de medical students dat if de Americans invading, de American flag she flying make *Nannette* and dem de enemy too. She tell de student to sit sweet, sweet, and to look like dey innocent. Den she go below and call de Grenadian coast guard on she radio. She tell dem dat *Nannette* all cleared to leave, den she ask de mon nice, nice, to notify de PRA at Fort Rupert above de harbor dat dey ain't suppose to shoot at de boat and she people.

"Well, de yacht leave de dock ten minutes before six. Bob come running over from he yacht to tell dem good-bye, and he really look sick, sick, because he boat up in de air on de dry dock like a target. As *Nannette* set off, Bob stood waving for a little while; he look like a lost chile, all helpless.

"Behind de wheel Miss Jilly trying to look cool, cool, and like she ain't scared to death. Dey pass safely around de jetties in Grenada Yacht Services. But when dey approaching de narrow cut between de lagoon and de Carenage, where de big ships dock, what you t'ink happen?"

"What?" whispered Miss Lucy, her eyes enormous...

Jilly paled as two Grenadian coast guard boats came through the cut and bracketed *Nannette.* The men on board motioned for her to stop the boat. The soldiers lined up on the decks of the boats were armed with AK-47s, all pointing at the students clustered in the cockpit. Jilly's knees knocked together so hard they would be bruised and sore for a week.

"Hi, guys," she called, trying to sound cheerful. "What's happening? Why are you stopping me?"

"Where you going, Miss Jilly?" one of them asked.

"I'm cleared for Union Island." She held her breath, and looked quickly below decks, where Peter Lucas was quietly going into the head. There the curtain was pulled across the porthole, and he could not be seen.

"Can you take us with you?" the skipper of one vessel called, laughing. "You know who in dose planes up dere? De Americans!"

"We wanted to show you we new uniforms," another man shouted good-naturedly. They all did a full turn, posing with their guns.

Jilly went dizzy with relief. She wondered if the men realized she had almost had a heart attack because of their fashion show. A frozen smile on her lips, she took several deep breaths and watched them.

They told her they were planning to take off the new uniforms and lay low, as they had no intention of fighting the Americans. They also warned her that it was rough as hell outside, and she was in for the sail of her life.

The people on *Nannette* called their thanks to the departing coast guard boats, and Jilly took the sloop out through the cut. They still had about half a mile to go before they were opposite Fort Rupert.

Suddenly the whole world seemed to erupt around them. Antiaircraft guns around St. Georges were firing every second.

From the American planes in the distance came a sound like a raspberry, of all things.

Laughing uproariously, Mike joked about how that sound must be a new kind of psychological warfare. "Every time the gunners miss, the Americans go *prrraaaccckkk!* I love it!" Later they learned that the sounds were made by Gatling guns, called Puff the Magic Dragon by the military...

"Mon, de yacht forge ahead; dere ain't any other place to go, just on into de battle!" Mr. Flowers raised his arm and pointed dramatically toward the roof. "See de fort up dere! And see me—*Nannette!* Just as dey directly opposite Fort Rupert, here come a set of noise like you ain't hear before— *wokwokwokwokwok!* And a wave of American helicopter—it look like a hundred of dem—come over de Morne. Dat a big mountain overlooking St. Georges, where Fort Frederick sit next to de mental asylum.

"Well, all kind of hell break loose! And den all dem antiaircraft gun in de trees along de coast go off like thunder rolling across de island! De medical students all mash together in de cockpit jumping up and down, up and down, and yelling for de helicopter to get de commie bastard!

"Miss Jilly look up at Fort Rupert and see de soldiers peering down at de boat, and den dey start firing all dem AK-47s at she, at de helicopter, at bird, and anyt'ing else dat move! Den she realize dat dey lowering de *big* gun to blow *Nannette* out de water!" Mr. Flowers turned and stared hard into the eyes of each listener. "You know what happen?"

Charlie laughed gently at the old man and nodded for Miss Lucy to pour another rum. "What, Lis Twa?"

"Mon, de eye of dat big gun look like a giant black hole when Miss Jilly stare into de t'ing—she t'ink of a mash-up boat and a set of dead floating in de water, and she one of dem. Den she see dem putting in de shell. Jilly yell at de students to sit down and shut dey arse!

"Den she steer close, close to de land under de fort, because she figure dat de bra—me ain't know de word—how de shell fall . . ."

"Trajectory," Charlie filled in.

"Yeah, de trajectory miss de boat. And she was right! Dey too close to de fort now—de gun couldn't hit dem—but de bad johns fire a shell over dey heads anyway. De shell land in de water on de other side, and de splash wet all de student. And den de medical student get sober, eh?

"Jilly sailing by, trying to look friendly while bullet falling into de water between she boat and de fort. She praying she going make it. She wave at de men in de fort, but dey just keep firing at de boat with de AK-47s like a set of *moko*." Mr. Flowers downed the rest of his drink and bowed a little to acknowledge the admiration in Miss Jilly's eyes. "Now, you tell de rest of de story, Miss Jilly..."

"Thank God they were lousy shots," Jilly told the small group in the rum shop. "The troops were firing the AK-47s down at us and had the angle wrong. The next day we heard that an American helicopter was shot down and crashed near the lagoon."

Mr. Flowers sighed, touched Charlie on the arm, and whispered, "Now pay attention, *garçon*, because she coming to de t'ing."

"We were motor-sailing, and the water was as choppy as I've ever seen it. Finally we rounded the point and were out of sight of Fort Rupert. I breathed a sigh of relief, then noticed that one of the American helicopters seemed to be chasing us. I could see a man with a megaphone leaning out, hailing us, gesturing for us to turn around.

"I screamed at him, asking what he wanted.

"The helicopter got closer, and through the *wok-wok-wok* from the rotors, I could hear the guy yelling that if I didn't turn back into port, he'd rip out my mast.

"My two objectives were to convince him that we were Americans and to get him to leave us alone. Going back meant almost certain death—there was no way I'd risk passing under Fort Rupert again. I pointed to the American flag and gestured toward the United Nations' burgee. The medical students waved at the men in the helicopter. But it did no good. The copter kept coming closer and dropped a wire to attack my mast."

Mr. Flowers leaned forward, intent on each word.

"What could I do to convince them I was an American? There had to be something! Frantic, I jumped up on the cockpit seat and made certain the guy in the helicopter could see me plainly, then I defiantly flipped him the bird.

"'Kay, ma'am . . . now I know you're an American,' he called over the loudspeaker.

"The helicopter turned and flew away, while Mike doubled over with laughter. We made it to Union Island just fine, and finally Peter got medical attention for his head wound. So you see, Mr. Prudhomme, I was saved by the bird."

Mr. Flowers looked confused. He turned to Charlie and cocked his head. "You see what I mean, Charlie? What is *flip him de bird?*"

Charlie laughed and extended his middle finger. "That is called 'the bird,' Lis Twa."

Mr. Flowers's mouth fell open. He looked at his hand, then extended his own middle finger and gasped. Eyes wide with shock, he stared at Jilly. "But you a lady! You—did dat? To a strange mon? *Eh-ehhhhhhhhh!*"

DIALOGUE

Charlie was walking down the path from the mountaintop to the main road. He felt glad the day was done. The sun had been incredibly hot; his brain felt roasted. Old mango trees cast long shadows over the verdant bush. The shade looked inviting, but the thought of reaching Miss Lucy's rum shop quickened his step.

"*Garçon!*"

He turned, wondering who was calling in such a familiar way, and saw that old Mr. Flowers was coming down the path just behind him.

"Eh-*eh,* bwoy, what you doing up here?" Mr. Flowers asked.

"We were surveying at the mountaintop today," the American explained. "There's some talk about building a new hotel, one that caters to people on special diets, in this part of the island. Do you live up here?"

"Yes, *garçon,* right beyond de bend you just passed. You know, I glad to see you here instead of at de rum shop. I have a legal problem and need some advice."

"Eh-eh, Mr. Flowers," Charlie teased, "woman after you? I'm not a lawyer. I'm an engineer."

"No woman don't bother me again," the old man replied seriously. "But it my nephew, Mangomon, from Castries. Of course, Mangomon he false name; he real name is Antonius Charles. He was here dis afternoon to get my advice, and I didn't know what to tell him. Let we sit here in de shade, and you tell me what to do."

They settled in deep shadow on the roots of an enormous African tulip tree. The old man took some time getting his bones comfortable, then stared off into space.

"My nephew have a serious problem. He want to know if he can sue Canada."

Charlie started. "He wants to do *what?*"

"He want to enter a paternity suit against Canada. I tell him I never hear of such a t'ing, and it certain no *mon* ever enter a paternity suit against anybody, 'specially a government."

"You're right there, my friend," Charlie remarked, laughing. "Does he live in Canada?"

"No, he live in Castries. But he insist dat Canada responsible for getting he outside woman pregnant, and he t'ink he have a good case."

The American mused. "Well, it would certainly be a first in the annals of the law."

"You mean it would set a president?"

"It certainly would! Uh, just how did a country get his outside woman pregnant? That might be a difficult concept for his attorney to explain to a jury."

The old man's eyes snapped with glee. "Well, Mangomon a big executive with one of de companies in Castries. He start out when he finish school dere, and work he way right up to de top. He smart, smart.

"Well, he have dis outside woman for years now, and he have three children by she. Den she get on about birth control and have sheself fix, or somet'ing. I don't really understand what medicine do to woman, eh? When I was young, you just make de baby, and dat is dat. But now t'ing all change up, change up. But de doctors tell she dat she can't get with child again."

The old man leaned back against the tree and stared at the shafts of light slanting through the foliage. "Mangomon see dis piece in de paper about how Canada going bring down soybean to de islands, to increase de amount of protein we eat. You know, it some kind of aid.

"Well, Mangomon been feeling poorly for some time because he working too hard. He decide to try dis soybean and see if it help how he feel. Den he hear some Rastas going on about how de soybean make a mon really strong, if you follow me. I mean, dey say de mon become a *real* mon when he eat dis soybean! Dey say soybean better for mon dan a whole heap of *lambie,* or cashew nut and t'ing!

"So Mangomon go on dis diet. He eat soybean bread, soybean mash up, soybean any way he can get it down! And he tell me dat he begin to feel good, good. He feel like a mon. He say he hardly control himself when he see a woman, de soybean give him so much strength.

"Bwoy, he say he working from early to late, trying to get rid of dat energy! He say he cut grass in a minute, clean out de shed in a second, go through he paperwork in a blink! He tell me he whole life speed up, speed up. He feel like he a youth again, *garçon,* and everyt'ing nice. But he have to show off to de outside woman, *oui?* He at she from morning till nightfall, *oui?* And now she pregnant, and Mangomon vex, *vex!* He say de soybean get de woman pregnant, and if Canada didn't bring it into de island he not be in trouble with he wife! Because she say dat three children by de outside woman more dan enough, and if he keep up de business, she mash he head, one time!"

Charlie laughed softly. Practicing law under the shady tree in just the same way that carpenters, furniture makers, and mechanics across the Caribbean practiced their trades in the cool shadows tickled his fancy. A shady tree attorney!

"So, what you t'ink?" Mr. Flowers asked.

"Well . . ." Charlie began.

"You t'ink he have a case?"

"I would say that it is impossible for a bean to impregnate a woman—"

"Mangomon say he t'ink he sue for a million Canadian dollar."

"—and that the jury would say that Mangomon, not the bean, impregnated the woman."

"Den, when he have de money, he going take me to Canada! You know, *garçon*, I never been out of de Caribbean in my life. I been to all de islands, even to Guyana, but—"

"Did you tell Mangomon what it will cost him to take this thing to court? He'll have to hire an attorney and get positive proof that the soybean made him more virile. I—"

"—never to Canada! You know I never see de snow fall? I hear it cold, cold, like angry woman, but soft, soft, like a chile."

"—don't think that can be proven. After all, if Mangomon didn't go at his woman morning and night, she would have stayed—"

"And Canada have building tall as tree! Even taller dan dis tree we sitting under, you know dat? Eh-*eh, garçon,* why you frowning so? You don't t'ink Mangomon have a case?"

"No, I don't think so, Mr. Flowers. You see, the law is peculiar in some ways, and I think it would be most peculiar in this way. I think Mangomon just better forget it."

Mr. Flowers shook his head. He was clearly disappointed. "Eh-eh, and me looking forward to going to Canada! Well, what you t'ink about going to Miss Lucy and having a rum? If I can't have Canada, you can buy me a rum."

"That, Mr. Flowers, can be very easily arranged."

They walked slowly down the path to the bottom of the mountain. By the time he and Charlie hit the road, the old man was nodding happily to the ladies they passed on the way.

YELLOWMAN

The sun had gone down; the air was beginning to cool somewhat. Charlie had worked late that evening and was just heading to the rum shop for a drink and some companionship when a voice called out from behind him. He turned, and there was old Mr. Flowers, hobbling along.

"Good evening, Mr. Flowers," he called. "Heading down to Miss Lucy's?"

"Evening, son," the elderly storyteller said breathlessly. "I figure you going to de rum shop, so I cotch you."

"You're welcome company, sir," Charlie replied.

On this evening Mr. Flowers's hat was bedecked with brilliant coral bougainvillea, which shimmered around the brim like a fiery halo in the gathering dusk.

The two men stepped through the rum shop door and were greeted by their usual companions.

Miss Lucy spied Mr. Flowers. "You have money this evening, Lis Twa, or a story?"

"Miss Lucy," the old man said, chuckling, "you know I never have any money. Where a mon ninety-two get money? But I have dis story."

Miss Lucy signaled for him to wait for a moment while she served several women who had come in for groceries to enjoy with their evening tea: corned beef, slices of cheese, bread, and sometimes a sweetie for a child. When she had completed the transactions, she joined the men at the bar and poured Mr. Flowers a white rum with a separate glass of water.

"What's the story about this evening, Lis Twa?" she asked.

Several children hanging about crept nearer to the bar and settled quiety around the walls to listen. Their eyes glowed in the soft light. Lis Twa was obviously their favorite adult; he was a much better teacher than those in school.

"Well, Miss Lucy, I tell you. All you remember dat mon who used to live down by Praslin? De mon call Yellowmon? Bwoy, Yellowmon was strange. He mooma, she black and have all kind of mix blood in she vein. And he poopa a white mon, and you know white mon have all kind mix up in him! You'd t'ink with all dis mix he get on all right, but Yellowmon grow up *racial! Bon Dieu,* if you see *racial!*

"Now, Yellowmon born with a kind of Chinee skin, smooth, pretty color, nice. Dat why he call Yellowmon. When he a bwoy, he wear he hair in a big Afro and talk about black power and t'ing. But when he turn mon, he go backways complete! Yellowmon don't want anyone to t'ink he black. No, no! Everyone must t'ink he a white mon, like it make any difference what color you skin is!

"You take my friend here," he said, pointing to Charlie. "He white, but he a mon just de same. He drink rum like any black mon; he turn he head like a black mon when pretty woman pass, and when he tired, he sleep just like a black mon." He smiled toothlessly at Miss Lucy and cleared his throat. "Oh, Miss Lucy, I dry!"

The woman winked at her customers and poured another round with alacrity. One of the men signaled that he would buy for Mr. Flowers, and Charlie did the same. They all enjoyed Lis Twa's stories tremendously. The children scooted closer, so as not to miss a word.

"Well, Yellowmon grow tall and strong," Mr. Flowers continued, "and he smart, smart, except for being so *racial.* He get job in de bank and go to England to study course and t'ing. Bwoy, when he get back, he look real strange, because he eye go funny.

"You remember how Yellow have dat nice slanty eye and high cheekbone from Africa? How he look like dose real tall African and have a handsome head? Well, Yellow have de fold take from he eyelid when he in England, and den he tell all he a Chinee! Who de hell ever hear of a *Chinee* named Braithwaite, I ask you? *Eh–eh!* Chinee have name like music, you know? Sing, Sung, Chong, Chan, Don, Chow, Chang, Ching.

His eyes shone with mischief. "All you children now learn Chinee names." He conducted them, using his walking stick as a baton, and they giggled and sang, "Sing, Sung, Chong, Chan, Don, Chow, Chang, Ching."

"But how any mon sing 'Braithwaite?" Mr. Flowers used the local pronunciation, Braffit. "It sound more like you clearing you throat or making a sneeze."

Everyone enjoyed a hearty laugh at that, then waited eagerly for Mr. Flowers to continue.

"Anyway, Yellowmon come back and go to work in de bank. He really good in dat work, you know, so he begin to move up de ladder of success, as dey say...."

Mr. Braithwaite cleared his throat judiciously and looked at the prospective borrower, a fellow he had known since childhood. "Just what do you want the money for, eh? You must tell me what you want the money for! Do you wish to buy a farm or a transport? I must have the information."

"Well, to tell de truth, Yellowmon—I mean Mr. Braithwaite, sah, I want to buy a transport." Donatus fidgeted uncomfortably beneath the unflinching gaze of those unfamiliar eyes.

Braithwaite softened his voice slightly. "You understand, don't you, that if the bank lends you the money, you must pay it back?"

"Well, yes, sah, I understand dat. But how much I have to pay back? Dey tell me some t'ing about—"

"Interest?"

"Yeah, dat de word."

Capricious Paradise

"Well, the bank charges you eighteen percent on what you borrow, which means that if you borrow thirty thousand dollars, you owe the bank eighteen percent on whatever balance is outstanding."

"Well, I must have de transport. De bananas ain't doing so good, so I decide to take up a taxi."

"In that case, all you have to pay back is five hundred dollars a month," Braithwaite explained patiently. No final figure would be mentioned. Truth in lending scared away customers; every banker in the Caribbean knew that...

"Like my friend Donatus taking on interest! He don't want to hear about dat; he want de money in hand to buy de transport."

"Mr. Flowers, I thought you were going to tell we a story!" one of the children complained.

"Chile, what going happen when you grow up and go in de bank, and you don't know about interest?" Mr. Flowers scolded jokingly. "You end up paying dem ten dollar for every ten dollar, dat's what!"

"No, no, Lis Twa. Me going school and study to be a farmer, and farmer don't need no transport," the child retorted, not to be outdone.

"Come, Mr. Flowers, come," Charlie urged. "We're all dying to know what happened to Yellowman."

Lis Twa wagged his finger at the smart-mouthed child, then continued. "Well, Yellow work hard, hard, and he don't have any *fete* and t'ing to take he mind off de work. So when finally he look up from de grindstone, what you t'ink happen?"

"What?" chorused all the children.

"Well, Yellow fall in love! He go to dis real fancy restaurant where all de tourist eat, because he don't want to eat around no native. He sitting dere like a king, de only black Chinee in de place, all dress up, dress up like he going to funeral, when de lash fall...."

The outer door opened, and a woman, followed by a customer of the bank, stepped through. She was tall and beautiful, with slanted eyes and hair that shone like a heaven full of stars.

Every head in the restaurant turned to watch this magnificent queen of Sheba. The man with her said something, and she smiled. Her smile lit up the restaurant like a sun.

Yellowman forgot his food. He could not swallow but sat there, mute, staring at the beauty before him. He dropped his fork with a clatter. The noise caught her attention, and curious, she looked at Yellowman and blinked. He was lost...

"She come in, and she escort—"

"What is a escort, Lis Twa?" asked a little girl.

"Well, escort is like, well, escort is a kind of—" The old man looked to his companions for help.

Charlie explained to the children that an escort was a gentleman who took a lady to dinner.

The children looked wise and informed.

"Anyway," Lis Twa went on, "she come in, and she escort follow, and dey seated at a table. Yellow can't take it on. He must know who de lady is, or he feel he gonna die. Now, he know de escort a little, so he rise and walk over to de table and say, all jolly and nice, 'Grolius, how nice to see you, mon. How are t'ings?'

"And Grolius, who doing some serious t'inking about borrowing money from de bank, smile and nod, and nod and smile. 'I fine, Mr. Braithwaite. How are t'ings at de bank?' He rise, shake Yellow's hand, and ask if Yellowmon know Miss Lydia Jean-Baptiste. She smile at Yellow, and he feel like he leg turn to water. With one smile de woman just melt de mon..."

Somehow Yellowman managed to make it home safely that night. He couldn't remember driving his latest pride and joy, a big Toyota. All the way to his house the luminous and inviting face of Lydia Jean-Baptiste hung on the night before him.

He slept not at all. Her beauty haunted him, taunted him with luscious lips and merry eyes. The next morning found him haggard from lack of sleep, but elated.

After a cup of tea, he reached for the telephone directory. There she was! Lydia Jn.Baptiste. She lived somewhere on the Morne. He could call her and ask her out. All he had to do was to ring her number and say a few words. But would she go out with him?—he wondered. What if his clothes weren't cut right, or if his hair was too long? Suppose she liked short men? Grolius was only five ten. He glanced down and grimaced. He had long, slender feet. Suppose she hated long, slender feet?

That morning at work he was a wreck. His hands shook; he developed a tic in his left eye. He even lent money to a known thief.

By that evening he had decided to call her. He felt fatalistic about it. All she could do was refuse his invitation...

"Den he take a big breath and take up de phone. 'Miss Jean-Baptiste?' he say, soft, soft. 'Dis is Theodore Braithwaite. We was introduced at Capone's by Mr. Grolius. I was wondering if you was free for dinner tomorrow?' He try to sound cool.

"'Oh, my, Mr. Braithwaite, how nice to hear from you! I'd love to have dinner with you. What time?'"

Mr. Flowers's falsetto struck Charlie and the others as uproariously funny. Miss Lucy wiped tears of laughter from her eyes.

"Well, Yellow feel like he head going bust! 'Ah, suppose I meet you around seven? You'll have to give me directions to your house.'

"'Oh,' she say, 'dat's easy. I live at Morne Fortune apartments, number fourteen.'

"Bwoy, Yellow now in a fix. If de woman live in dose apartments, it mean she ain't a local gal! It mean she come from somewhere else, and if she go away, Yellow can't abide St. Lucia no more without she! De place look a desert one time, and he going die of thirst. 'Fine, den,' he say, 'I'll see you tomorrow evening. I look forward to it.'

"She say good-bye and hang up. Yellow in a sweat. He knee shake, and he hand tremble, and he trying hard to cotch de breath. Bwoy, love is a terrible t'ing for some folk."

Mr. Flowers looked up and grinned. He stretched, then glanced at the children. They were staring at him, hypnotized.

"Next evening Yellow find out dat Miss Lydia from Jamaica, and she have some kind of fancy work; she librarian for a set of computer or somet'ing, and she in St. Lucia for a consultancy."

"What a consultancy, Lis Twa?" called one of the children.

"Well, dat when you know more dan I know about somet'ing, so I call you to tell me about it. I ask you all kind of question, and you give me all kind of answer, and I pay you for de answer."

That seemed to satisfy the children, and they settled back. Miss Lucy poured another round for all, and Mr. Flowers downed his rum and followed it with a glass of water. He then shook himself and got back to business.

"Well, de bottom fall out of Yellow world. He know den dat Miss Lydia going be gone before long, and he ain't see she again 'cause she going all de way back to Jamaica!

"Bwoy, de courtship begin! Yellow almost bury de woman under flower. He send she wine and coconut lovebird. He feed de woman so many meal in fancy restaurant it surprising she ain't get fat. Yellow cannot get enough of dis woman name Lydia! He a change mon! De bank don't get nothing but he body during de day because he t'inking about Miss Lydia.

"But dere is one t'ing dat Yellowmon don't see about Miss Lydia. It like he blind. De woman black as a eggplant! She dat beautiful purply black just like melogen! All Yellow friend really surprise, knowing how racial Yellow is. But he don't see at all. And he getting desperate because de consultancy drawing to a close.

"One night when de moon full and light up de island like a white sun, Yellow take himself in hand and tell Miss Lydia dat he love she. Dey down by Reduit on de beach, strolling back and forth like tourist in de moonlight. Yellow heart beating, a steel drum in a calypso. It shaking he body.

"Miss Lydia look up at Yellow and tell him dat she really fond of him. And what you t'ink Yellow do? He ask she to marry him!

Capricious Paradise

"'Oh, Theodore, I am touch,' she say." Mr. Flowers's voice melted and sighed.

"'I could make you very happy, Lydia,' he say.

"And den de cutlash fall. She tell him dat she never marry anyone who ain't a black mon. She say how she always believe dat black should stick to black, and white to white, and Chinee to Chinee. She tell Yellow she sorry she so racial, but she always been dat way, and never, never would she marry a Chinee, because he ain't black.

"'But I am a black mon!' Yellow howl.

"'Oh, Theodore, I wish I could believe dat, but your eye give de lie. You have real Chinee eye, and dey give you away. Forgive me, please?' She kind of sigh. And de next day, she gone back to Jamaica!"

"What happen to poor Yellowmon?" asked one of the children.

"Oh, he apply for transfer, and dey send him to someplace to work in de bank. He ain't never come back to St. Lucia except for holiday," Lis Twa explained.

"And what is the moral of that story, Mr. Flowers?" Miss Lucy asked brightly, eyeing the children.

"Well, it mean dat being racial stupid, Miss Lucy. De wheel always come full circle."

They all agreed to that. Race is, after all, only skin-deep. Mr. Flowers smiled at his audience, then waved good night and started to leave.

Charlie picked up his hat and called to Mr. Flowers as he went out the door. They walked quietly for a while together in the dusk—black man, white man—friends.

THE FATHER OF HIS COUNTRY

The rum shop was unusually full of children, all in a holiday mood. They were dressed in their Sunday best, with braids gleaming, shoes shined, ruffles starched, and ribbons everywhere. Even the older boys and girls, some of whom already held jobs, were in attendance. Miss Lucy was frantic, hurrying up and down behind the counter and serving Cokes, Juicys, Icys, and penny candies.

Once the children were served, they went outside to join their mothers, who milled about in the yard outside Miss Lucy's. Gossiping and taking stock of one another, as women will do on certain occasions, they too were in their best clothes, generally of lace or satin. The yard resembled a flower stall, but a divided one. There were two distinct groups of mothers and offspring, each eyeing the other, and while everyone was polite, there was a certain tension in the air. The conspicuous difference between the two groups was the ages of the children and young folk. One contingent was much younger than the other and ranged in age from infants through ten-year-olds; the other cluster encompassed offspring from babes to mature men and women. The mothers of both groups, however, included toothless grandmothers and nubile females in their first bloom.

It was just on five in the afternoon, and the Americans had knocked off work a bit early because the prime minister, Flavius Primrose, was due to debate the leader of the Opposition in the village that day. The two politicians had been at each other hammer and tongs for some weeks, and the Americans, as foreigners, were curious to hear the disputation.

The island was in the throes of electioneering. Church leaders and schoolmasters, contractors and merchants, all had their day in the sun, appearing on television in quivering commercials for the candidate of their choice. Naturally the blurbs by the Opposition were somehow jerkier, obscured by faults in local technology; but that was to be expected.

"Eh-eh, *garçon,* what all you doing here?"

Charlie turned, and there was old Mr. Flowers, his donkey-eared hat for once unadorned. "Mr. Flowers," he said, surprised, "I didn't see you."

"Bwoy, dere so many hats here today, I invisible. You ever see such going on? Look all dem women, dress up, dress up, like is church dey going to! Eh-eh."

Charlie and another American, Dana Martin, a Peace Corps volunteer, drew Mr. Flowers aside, away from the shifting crowd. "Why are the people standing in two distinct groups?" Charlie asked.

"Well, it according to who dey are, *garçon.* Some of dem belong to Delaware Champfleur, de leader of de Opposition, but most of dem belong to de prime minister." He cocked his head to one side and studied his friends carefully, assessing their willingness to buy rum. "You mean all you don't know how de prime minister stay in power so long?"

"I assume it is because he's a good leader," Dana, in his innocence, replied.

A quick glance showed that the crowd in the rum shop had thinned by now; everyone had his drink or candy, and most had joined their mothers under the trees lining the road. Charlie led the way into the bar to join several of his colleagues, and he, Dana, and Mr. Flowers greeted Miss Lucy, who looked rather harried.

"Miss Lucy," the old man said, cackling and pointing at Dana, "de mon here t'ink de prime minister stay in power because he a good leader."

"*Eh–ehhhh!*" was Miss Lucy's comment. "You want a rum, Mr. Flowers?"

"Yeah, Miss Lucy, if de gentlemon be so kind."

Charlie nodded agreement, and Miss Lucy served them. She leaned tiredly over the counter and studied Mr. Flowers, then grinned at the mischief shining in the old man's eyes. "Well, Mr. Flowers, I'll bet we can persuade you to explain the prime minister's secret to our American friends."

"Dat I can, Miss Lucy." He turned to Charlie. "*Garçon,* I tell you de story of island politics," Mr. Flowers began. "I never knew dat all you not familiar with de way t'ings done around here. Miss Lucy, how old you t'ink de prime minister is today?"

"I know he's in his seventies," she replied. "But just how far along, I'm not sure."

"De mon seventy-seven year old!" Mr. Flowers cried. "You know how many year dat give him to make child? Sixty year and some, dat how long he have to make child. And poor Champfleur, de leader of de Opposition, he only fifty-nine, so he lost, lost.

"Now, I know Flavius Primrose since he a bwoy. He was a smart bwoy, and ambitious. When he just ten he make up he mind dat he going to become de leader of he country, and decide den to make de sacrifice necessary to reach he goal.

"Dat in de days when dere ain't no chance of black mon ever running de country, you understand. In dose days England rule over all de islands and have governor for each country, and all we kept apart. Dat de British way, divide and rule, and dat's what dey did in de islands here in de Caribbean." He downed his rum and chased it with water, then licked his lips.

"Bwoy, you t'ink it easy to become prime minister? Mon must go from morning till de night fall, and far into de night, to be prime minister.

"Now, Flavius come from a good island family, and dey run a little store in de country, with dry goods, rum shop, lumber, and t'ing, so dey have a little money put aside for Flavius's education. And he smart, smart. Mon, he end up going to

Capricious Paradise

England to de university, and he get a degree in somet'ing call political science."

The old man laughed gleefully. "You see how wicked dem politicians are? Dey not content just making de people a fool. Dey make a *science* out of fooling de people! You ever hear so? Bwoy, all dem real scamp, *oui*?"

Dana bought Mr. Flowers another rum, and while he drank it, the Americans peered outside. The crowd had grown larger, with even more mothers and their children joining the two groups. Good-natured banter flew back and forth in the soft evening air.

"Well," Lis Twa continued, "Flavius begin on he plan even before he leave for de university. He make two baby when he sixteen, and three baby when he seventeen. In he eighteenth year, when he leaving for England, he make *eight* baby!"

"Uh—what was the point in making all the children, Lis Twa?" one of the Americans asked. "I don't see the connection between making babies and—"

"Bwoy, who going vote for you?" Mr. Flowers looked with pity at his friend. "T'ink, mon! *Who going vote for you? You family, dat's who!*"

"Good grief," Charlie muttered, shocked, "you're saying that—"

"You see how smart Flavius is? Long before he able to run for office—years before de islands get dey own premier and dey own government—dat boy t'inking!

"Well, when he return from de university, he really buckle down and get busy making babies. Every woman on de island who have teeth in she mouth and young enough to have chile have chile by Flavius. De bwoy almost kill himself making baby. He work at it day and night, night and day, until he ready to drop.

"And he work hard at de family business, so he can send every child a sweetie when dey birthday come around. You see hard work? Dat hard work! But it good for de business because all de women he give baby to t'ink he special. And dey know he t'ink dey special as well. So dey call at de store and buy from Flavius.

"Mon, de business grow so big dat Flavius now almost rich. He bring in car and start to sell it and den bring in machine to make de cement block so people don't have to make dem by hand to build dey house. When he prime minister and put electricity out in de country, he bring in washing machine and television, so he can sell to de moomas of he children.

"And, mon, when de lady come in to buy she little t'ing, Flavius have she in he office, give she a cup of tea or a rum, and what you t'ink he do dere?"

"What?" Charlie questioned.

"He make another baby while de woman rest from she shopping!" Mr. Flowers announced triumphantly.

There was a loud cheer from one group outside as the leader of the Opposition arrived in his Mercedes to address his people. As Delaware Champfleur descended from the auto, Charlie could see that he was an enormous man, built like a bull but with a simian head. The politician dived into the smaller group, where he shook hands, kissed cheeks, smiled, and nodded.

The children crowded around him. One could hear cries and murmurs, which sounded mightily to Charlie like "Poopa."

"You see dat mon?" Mr. Flowers asked, regaining their attention, "He a amateur. He almost thirty when he decide he going into politics. He don't start making baby except on he wife and he one outside woman till den. You see me? I never vote for him, never, because de mon don't t'ink ahead!

"Delaware raise in de country, in a shack like de one I live in. He family poor, poor, but dey proud. He poopa work hard, hard on de estate run by Mistress Skinner, to send Delaware to school. De poopa chop weed, mash tree, plant banana, and dig ditch to send dat boy to school. But he ain't smart. Dat a real shame, mon work so hard, and he son stupid, stupid.

"Well, Delaware get through de sixth form, and den he poopa die from all dat hard work. So he have to leave school and help he mooma feed de rest of de children. He get a job in one of Flavius's store and clerk for ten year, den he go into business on he own. All dat work he do for Flavius teach him how to run shop, so he do he own t'ing.

"By dat time, he getting idea about all kind of t'ing, like how de farmer deserve a little help and how de poor mon need a hospital—all dem t'ings—but it don't get him nowhere. He just a shop mon; he no politician. But he start preaching in de country about how de poor not getting dey shake and such, and people start talking about how good a mon he is. *Eh-eh!*

"You see how de mon stupid? All he do when he in de country is *talk!* He ain't make no baby; he ain't take no sweetie to de woman of de house. De mon a real *moko!*

"Den he decide to take de big step and run against Flavius in election. Well, who tell him try dat? De mon lose one time—*braps!*—and fall on he face. He only get four thousand vote in de whole country because everyone a stranger.

"Dat when he get smart and begin making baby, but he years behind de prime minister. You see dat little group dere, greeting him? See how all dem young? Dat all he done here in de south of de island. I hear he have more children in de north, but if you gonna win de election, you must have family all over, *oui?*

"Some of those women are really, uh—" Charlie hesitated.

"Ugly?" asked Miss Lucy, laughing at the expression on the American's face.

"Well, yes."

"Eh-eh, *garçon,* you t'ink only pretty woman vote? Dat where de prime minister really shine. He make baby on everyone—pretty, ugly, even dem dat need bag over dey head. De ugly woman always grateful and talk about how big a mon de prime minister is. You see how de mon smart, smart!"

There was an enormous cheer outside, so they all stepped through the door to watch the prime minister's arrival. He was a short, dapper fellow, with a winning smile and thinning hair.

He jumped from his car and threw both hands into the air. The larger crowd went wild with cries of "Show dem, Poopa!" and "Let de speech begin!"

All the ladies rushed him, then touched him tenderly and grinned like contented cats as he circled among them, giving a kiss here and a pat there and throwing an affectionate arm across an elderly shoulder.

He glanced toward the rum shop and spied the foreigners. His eyes turned icy. Then he looked away and smiled warmly again at his people.

"Bwoy," Mr. Flowers remarked quietly, "you see how he turn it on and off? All you ain't voters, so dere ain't no use wasting a smile on you, eh? And you see how tired de mon look, how he got black smudge under he eye? Well, dat from all de baby making. He too old now, but he still try."

"Mr. Flowers," Charlie said, puzzled, "hasn't he ever run out of women? I mean, after all the ladies have babies and grow older, where do the new babies come from?"

"Mon, dey come from de pickney!" Mr. Flowers told him.

"But isn't that—um—incest?"

"Incess, recess, progress, what it matter? De mon want to stay in power." The old man's eyes grew misty. "You know, *garçon*, I always admire Americans. And you first president—what he name?"

"You mean George Washington?" Dana asked.

"Yeah, he de one! De father of he country. Bwoy, when you t'ink how *big* dat country is and how many women it have—*bon Dieu!*—de chap musta been a *giant!*"

The End

ABOUT THE AUTHOR

Gilliam Clarke lived in the Caribbean—Trinidad, Grenada, and St. Lucia—for some fifteen years. She is married to a retired United Nations official. She was in Grenada during the invasion of Reagan's forces, and two of the stories are based on her experience during that time.

During her stay in St. Lucia she wrote a newspaper column on agriculture and history under the byline O. MacDonald.

All the stories are based on real events, with the exception of Nature Lovers, which tells of a Lucian myth, Le Gran Lezard.

A native of Washington, North Carolina, she worked in medicine, banking, and money management. She and her husband presently live in Southern Pines, North Carolina.

Printed in the United States
82680LV00008B/17/A